D1575841

First Day on Campus

"You must be Nancy," a cheerful voice said. "I'm Kara. Since you weren't here, I took the bed by the window because I'm a little claustrophobic. That *is* the rule of the dorm. First come, first pick."

"That's great," Nancy said quickly, even though she was a little disappointed.

Just then Eileen came into the room. With her was a girl cradling a computer keyboard in her arms. "Hey, Nancy, this is my roomie, Reva," Eileen announced.

"Does anyone have a flashlight?" Stephanie called out from across the hall. "I lost an earring under my bureau."

Suddenly the whole suite was in Nancy's room, with everyone talking at once. "And it's only noon," Nancy murmured to herself.

Well, college was going to be interesting, living with so many other people. Everyone was so different.

Isn't this what you wanted, though? Nancy reminded herself. What you tried to explain to Ned—the full college experience you need to try? So now that you have it, you'd better just hope it works!

Nancy Drew
on campus™ #1

New Lives, New Loves

Carolyn Keene

AN ARCHWAY PAPERBACK
Published by POCKET BOOKS
New York London Toronto Sydney Tokyo Singapore

AN ARCHWAY PAPERBACK *Original*

An Archway Paperback published by
POCKET BOOKS, a division of Simon & Schuster Inc.
1230 Avenue of the Americas, New York, NY 10020

Copyright © 1995 by Simon & Schuster Inc.
Produced by Mega-Books, Inc.

ISBN: 0-671-52737-1

First Archway Paperback printing September 1995

10 9 8 7 6 5 4 3 2 1

NANCY DREW, AN ARCHWAY PAPERBACK and colophon are registered trademarks of Simon & Schuster Inc.

NANCY DREW ON CAMPUS is a trademark of Simon & Schuster Inc.

Cover photos by Pat Hill Studio

Printed in the U.S.A.

IL 8+

PROLOGUE

Wilder University!" Nancy Drew pointed to the passing sign, her blue eyes sparkling. "I guess that makes us Wilder Girls," she said with a big smile, turning to her two best friends, Bess Marvin and George Fayne.

"That's Wilder W-o-m-e-n, Nancy—assuming we ever get there," George called out from the backseat of Nancy's Mustang. "I wouldn't count on it with Bess driving!"

"Hey!" Bess snapped, squinting into the rearview mirror. "What's wrong with my driving?"

"For one thing, you're staring at me and not at the red light ahead of us," George pointed out.

"Oops!" Bess lowered her eyes quickly to find the car in front of her at a standstill, and hit the brakes. As the Mustang jerked to a halt, the small luggage trailer they'd rented fishtailed. Bess winced and glanced apologetically at Nancy.

"Way to go, Bess." George rolled her eyes.

"Don't give her such a hard time," Nancy said. "I'm glad it's Bess's turn to drive. It's nice to sit back and be chauffeured for a change."

"Hey, what's that?" Bess asked, trying to read a handmade sign tacked to a tree.

" 'If You Thought You Knew...' " Nancy read as they drove past.

"There's another one," George cried, leaning over the front seat.

" 'What Wild Was...' " Nancy continued.

"There's one more at the corner," Bess said, squinting.

"That's where you turn right," George reminded her.

" 'Welcome to...' " Nancy read, a smile tugging at her lips, her blue eyes flashing.

The car rounded the corner onto a wide tree-lined street. Before them was an enormous sign.

" 'Wilder University!' " they all shouted in unison.

The steeple of the university's chapel peeked out above the trees. Beyond it Nancy could make out the Gothic slate roofs and brick facades of the classroom buildings she had toured on her visit last spring. Excitement rippled through her. She turned over the Wilder University brochure she was holding so she could follow their progress on the small map printed on the back.

"At the next light, turn right, go up the hill, and follow the signs," Nancy said.

After rolling down the window, she rested her elbow on the sill and lowered her chin onto her arm. Her long red-blond hair fluttering in the breeze, she stared at the passing town. The streets were clean and wide, and the houses were a jumbled collection of old Victorians. They passed a small organic food co-op, a diner, a used bookstore, and a Laundromat.

The roads were clogged with hundreds of university students, honking horns, waving out windows, dashing across streets to deliver welcoming hugs.

Finally they crested a hill and saw a huge open gate and a sign saying Wilder University, Est. 1902.

Bess leaned on the horn and joined the honking of the other cars as they drove through the university gates.

Nancy felt another surge of excitement. That morning she and her friends had left behind everything that was familiar.

She wasn't just visiting her boyfriend Ned Nickerson at Emerson College, as she'd done so many times. Wilder was *her* school now, and she was here to stay.

Glancing around, she realized that the campus was even prettier than she remembered it. When she'd come to visit in the early spring, it had been cold and muddy. But now, at the end of the summer, the high, arched trees cast dappled patterns of shade and light over the streets. Sunlight shone on the pale granite facades of the buildings. Students in shorts and tank tops clogged the walkways, talking and laughing. It was all so beautiful and so full of promise.

"Wow," George said from the backseat, taking in everything. "This is the beginning of the rest of our lives."

"I was just thinking the same thing." Nancy smiled to herself.

Just then three guys stepped off the curb right in front of the car. As they crossed the street, they peered inside the Mustang. When they saw the three girls, they smiled, flashing three sets of orthodontist-perfect white teeth.

"Excuse me while I just sit here a minute and watch them," Bess said with a sigh.

"I wonder if you're ever going to do any studying." George laughed, shaking her head.

"Studying?" Bess echoed. "That's easy. I'll just sign up for whatever classes those three are taking."

"At least then we'll know you'll go every day," George teased. "You really are too much, Bess. College is the time to think about your future."

"I am," Bess said.

George moaned, rolling her eyes. "Not just your *dating* future, Bess. I swear, sometimes even I have a hard time believing we're related."

It was true, Nancy mused fondly. No one would ever imagine Bess and George were first cousins. It wasn't just their personalities that were different, they didn't look alike, either.

George was tall, slim, and athletically graceful. She had dark eyes and softly curling brown hair, while Bess was all blond hair, blue eyes, and curves.

"Well, you know what they say," Nancy reminded them. "Opposites attract. And I'm just glad we were all attracted to the same school."

"Even if we're not roommates," Bess threw in, making a pouty face. "I still don't understand why you didn't want us to room together. We could have tried for a triple. It's because I'm such a slob, isn't it? You can tell me the truth."

"Oh, Bess." Nancy chuckled, shaking her head. Inside, though, she felt a twinge of guilt. Although Bess was one of her best friends, Nancy had to admit that Bess didn't have any organizational skills.

That wasn't the reason Nancy had wanted to be on her own, though. College for her was about discovery: new ideas, new places, and new people. Nancy loved Bess and George. The three of them would always be close, but Nancy didn't want to start out college life hiding behind their easy and comfortable friendship.

She knew George felt the same way. Living with other people didn't mean that they were deserting one another. They'd tried to explain their reasoning to Bess, but she hadn't really understood. Nancy knew that deep down Bess was still a little hurt about their decision to split up.

George cleared her throat in the small silence. "Speaking of us all going to Wilder," she began, "how did you leave things with Ned, Nan? Is he still upset about your not going to Emerson?"

"We didn't have a fight or anything," Nancy replied, squinting into the distance. "But when I said goodbye to him, he acted a little weird. He kept making cracks about how I'd forget him and find someone new."

"But you want to major in journalism," George argued. "Everyone knows that Emerson doesn't have a good journalism school. You had to come to Wilder. It has one of the best journalism departments in the country."

Nancy nodded, but inside she knew that she'd also picked Wilder for a more complicated reason.

Nancy had been to Emerson so many times to visit Ned that she didn't think of it as a place that could be hers. Because of Ned, she knew who the best teachers were, which classes were easy, and what fraternities and sororities had the best parties. There would be hardly anything left to discover, and Nancy wanted to experience college for herself. If she went to Emerson, she knew she'd be walking in Ned's shadow.

"Well, I'm sure he said those things because he'll miss you," Bess said.

"I guess he will," Nancy agreed. "But when I tried to explain why it was the right decision for me, he just didn't seem to get it. Sometimes I have the feeling he'd be happier if everything stayed the same forever. He just doesn't want to admit that life changes."

"Poor guy," Bess said softly. "I mean, you're

right, Nan, of course, but still . . . I can understand how he feels."

Nancy reached up to her throat and fingered the gold, heart-shaped locket Ned had given her as a going-away gift. He said it was to remind her of him always. All he'd talked about the last few weeks of summer was how most of the couples he knew had drifted apart once they were in separate colleges.

Nancy had tried to reassure him that she could never forget. She'd promised that the distance wouldn't come between them and reminded him that their love had survived his first two years in college. He made her promise never to take off the locket anyway, and she hadn't.

"Which dorm are you in again Nan," George asked, leaning forward.

"Thayer," Nancy replied, glad to get her mind off Ned.

She checked another brochure in her lap. "It's the newest one on campus." She raised her eyes and caught a glimpse of her Y-shaped dorm approaching on the right.

"I hope our dorm won't be an ancient ruin," Bess joked to George.

"Let me see that brochure," George said, snatching it from Nancy's hands. "Hey, Nan, your dorm may be new, but did you check out the layout of the suites? There's only one bathroom for eight of you."

Bess gasped in mock horror.

"What's wrong with that?" Nancy asked.

"That's eight girls per sink," George said.

"Eight girls per *mirror*," Bess said, clucking her tongue.

"So, what do you guys have in your dorm, your own Jacuzzi?" Nancy shot back.

"Didn't the brochure say our private bathrooms were *palatial*, Bess?" George said haughtily.

"I think the word was *luxurious*," Bess replied.

"All right, cut it out." Nancy laughed good-naturedly. "Hey, there's my dorm!" she cried, her spirits rising.

George whistled. "I take it all back, Nan," she said, taking in the modern brick building. "It looks great."

There were shiny brass columns at the front entrance flanking huge glass doors. The effect was a little like that of a fancy hotel. Each black window frame was fitted with a natural-colored shade.

"It's lucky for you, you get dropped off first," George pointed out. "Bess's mountain of luggage will take forever to unload."

"I didn't take *that* much." Bess sniffed.

"Don't get mad," Nancy said gently. "We love you even though you travel heavier than a freight train."

Nancy almost didn't wait for the car to stop before she opened the door and leaped out. She stood by the car, one hand resting on the roof for support while she pulled each of her long legs up in a runner's stretch behind her back to get rid of the cramps.

George climbed out of the backseat and threw her arms over her head to stretch also. "I think I'm jealous," she said, peering at Thayer Hall.

Nancy walked to the trailer attached to the back of the car and untied one corner of the tarp they'd stretched over their belongings. She yanked out two large suitcases, a tote bag, a backpack, and a desk lamp from home.

"Okay," she cried, banging on the hood of the car as she leaned down at the side window to say goodbye to Bess and George. "Wish me luck."

"You've never needed luck in your life, Nancy Drew." Bess smiled at her.

Nancy's eyes sparkled as she laughed. "Thanks, Bess, but I think that this time I'll take some just to be safe."

CHAPTER 1

Blowing a wisp of hair out of her eyes, Nancy adjusted the straps of her backpack, yanked the tote bag onto her shoulder, grabbed one of her suitcases by the handle, and struggled up the steps, leaving her other suitcase and the lamp at the side of the walkway with the other luggage and boxes lined up there. "Well, Thayer, here I am," she said under her breath as she entered the dorm that would be her home for the next year.

Just past the glass doors was a large lobby with a tiled floor and a bank of shiny silvery metal elevators. Along the walls were scattered bulletin boards covered with masses of brightly colored papers announcing events and gatherings for the upcoming week: Thayer Hall Orientation, Zeta Psi Freshman Bash, Asian-American Students Union . . .

There's so much to do! Nancy thought. When is there time for classes?

She was about to turn away when something on a board caught her eye.

LOOKING FOR A "WILDER TIME"?
THE *WILDER TIMES* WANTS *YOU!*
Wilder's Newspaper Is Looking for New Staff!
Come to the Organizational Meeting,
Wednesday, 8 P.M.
241 Goldwin Hall.

I'll be there, Nancy thought excitedly. She snatched up her suitcase. But it's only Saturday, she reminded herself. I've got to take college one step at a time. I'll start by finding my room.

Thayer Hall had five stories, with the dining hall and mail room on the first floor, and then alternating floors for freshmen men and women. Nancy's suite was on the third floor, so she started for the elevators. When she saw the lines of people waiting at each one, she shook her head and decided to climb the stairs. She fought a fluttery feeling in her stomach as she struggled up every step.

I don't know why I'm so worried, she thought. After all, I've been in hundreds of really nerve-wracking situations. Why should the first day of college make me so nervous?

Nancy stepped out into the third-floor hall and found herself confronted with three sets of doors—one for each wing of the Y-shaped building. She was in Suite 301, in the wing just to the right of the elevators and the stairway.

A little hesitantly, Nancy opened the door and found herself in a small lounge. Blue sofas and armchairs were grouped around a low round coffee table piled with university brochures, information pamphlets, and take-out menus from different pizzerias and Chinese restaurants. A short hallway branched off this room. It was lined with doors, and the hallway was jammed with girls, parents, and luggage. Everyone was twisting around to get in and out of rooms. Blowing away the same annoying piece of hair, Nancy put on a patient smile, lowered her shoulder, and plunged into the crush.

"Hey there!" a squarely built girl with freckles called out to her, shouting to be heard above the din. She bounded over to where Nancy stood. "Are you my roommate?"

"I don't know," Nancy answered. "Are you Kara Verbeck?"

"Nope," the girl said cheerfully, shaking her head. "Eileen O'Connor. Oh, well, I guess we're suitemates anyway. What's your name?"

"Nancy Drew," she answered.

"So let's get right to the important stuff," Eileen demanded. "Do you have a boyfriend?"

"What?" Nancy replied, startled by the abrupt question. "Well, actually, yes, I do."

"Lucky you, then." Eileen sighed. "You're preequipped. I guess that means you'll be getting actual schoolwork done this semester. Unlike me. That's the bane of us single animals," Eileen explained. "We always end up getting bad grades the first semester because we spend all our time scouring the campus for love." She laughed heartily.

Nancy couldn't help laughing with her. Eileen had a good sense of humor.

Maybe I should introduce her to Bess, Nancy thought. They could go "scouring the campus for love" together.

"You said you're rooming with Kara, right?" Eileen asked. "She's here already. You two are in the second room on the left."

"I'm definitely ready to drop this stuff." Nancy glanced down at her bags, which were growing heavier by the second. There was that flutter again. This time it was provoked by the thought of meeting the girl she'd be living with for the next year.

"That's the bathroom," Eileen continued, nodding toward an open door. "It's not as bad as it looks in the brochure. There's room for three of us in there at a time."

"Thanks," Nancy replied, laughing. I can't wait to tell George, she thought.

"Phone company. Phone company, coming through!" someone warned. A thin guy in a coverall barreled through, practically flattening everyone against the wall. He was wearing a leather holster; but instead of guns in the slots, he was packing phones, wires, and tools. He had a harried look, as if this was the hundredth crowded suite he'd had to fight through that day.

"All right, people, listen up," he declared hurriedly above the noise, though Nancy thought she was the only one listening. "The phones in your rooms don't work yet. No private service until next week. You can receive calls on the lounge phone, but if you want to make a call, you'll have to go downstairs to the pay phones. Any questions?" Not waiting for an answer, he shouted, "Good."

The door to the main hall slammed behind him, and he was gone.

"What a drag," Nancy heard someone say. She turned and found herself staring into the lovely brown eyes of a girl her height. Though not exactly beautiful, the girl appeared sophisticated, with her high cheekbones and bright red lipstick. She wore a white, low-cut bodysuit that showed off her slender figure and deep tan. Everything, from her expensive-looking haircut to her perfectly manicured nails, said "money."

"You pay gobs of money for tuition and room and board, and you don't even get a lousy phone," the girl complained in a lazy drawl.

Nancy smiled politely and tried to squeeze by. Since she was the one loaded down with luggage, Nancy thought the girl would step back to give her more room. She didn't budge an inch, however. Finally, Nancy just dropped her bags.

"Sorry about that," Nancy said, determined to be nice. "I'm Nancy Drew."

The girl arched an eyebrow at Nancy and smiled smugly. "Stephanie Keats," she said finally. "Excuse me." She brushed past Nancy and moved toward the lounge.

Nancy stared after her for a moment, taken aback. What's her problem? she wondered. Whatever it is, at least I can be thankful *she's* not my roommate.

Bess backed clumsily into the crammed elevator in Jamison Hall, clutching a green garbage bag stuffed with sweaters and socks. "Just one more load and I'm done," she whispered under her breath, thinking of the two suitcases sitting on the sidewalk outside and the last bits and pieces in the trailer.

"Thanks a lot, George," she mumbled again. Bess knew she shouldn't be mad, but she couldn't help feeling deserted by her cousin. George had brought only a third as much stuff as Bess, and as soon as she had finished unpacking, she bolted. George had said she wanted to wander around campus and check things out. She wouldn't wait even five minutes to help Bess up with her stuff.

I guess she's just excited, Bess explained to herself. I can't really blame her. There's so much to do, so much to see.

As Bess eyed the kids standing with her in the elevator, she felt overwhelmed by the newness of it all. Everyone was chatting, introducing themselves, comparing notes on their rooms. But somehow, all the noise and hubbub was reassuring. The kids she passed nodded hello. All the incoming freshmen like her seemed eager to be friends.

The elevator doors slid open on the second floor, and Bess stumbled out and staggered down the hall to Room 214.

As she stood catching her breath in the doorway, she smiled with relief.

"I really love it," she said out loud, setting down the bag of clothes. Her room was the one definitely great thing about college so far. It was light and airy, with decorative moldings around the high ceiling. Two twin beds sat under a large window, a small antique-looking nightstand separating them. Along each of the side walls were a built-in dresser, a wardrobe with mirrored doors, and a desk.

Nancy's dorm may be shiny and new, Bess thought, but mine has character.

Then Bess noticed a perfectly stacked pyramid of blue suitcases on the left-hand bed. Obviously, her roommate had arrived but wasn't in the room.

I hope we get along, Bess thought, glancing uneasily at what looked to her like a display for a luggage store. Then her heart dropped a little when she noticed two milk crates filled with books piled next to the suitcases.

"Oh, great," Bess mumbled. "She's already thinking about classes."

She leaned over to read the titles. *"Topics in Biochemistry,"* she read aloud, wrinkling her nose. "Ugh, sounds awful. Well, that's her life, not mine."

In truth, Bess was more than a little worried about studying. All through the application process, her parents had never stopped talking about how academically challenging college would be, and how she would have to work really hard applying herself as her cousin George did. George had always been a good student, and Bess knew that she personally hadn't a single academic gene in her body.

Bess was ready for parties and dances and football games—all the really great stuff she'd looked forward to since high school. But books? Classes? Tests? Studying all night? The concepts made her shudder.

"Party now, worry later," Bess said under her breath as she bounded cheerfully across the airy room and headed back into the hall for the last of her things. As she walked down the stairs, she glanced out the window and caught sight of George leaning against Nancy's blue Mustang, tapping her foot impatiently. "Uh-oh," Bess muttered, racing down the last few steps to retrieve the last of her things from the trailer.

At the front door, she barreled into a tall, preppy girl dressed in a green single-pocket T-shirt and tan chinos. "Sorry," Bess mumbled, rubbing her nose.

"You should be," the girl scolded, pursing her lips. Then she turned and headed for the bank of elevators.

Too bad everyone can't be friendly, Bess thought as she watched the girl disappear behind the closing doors of a jammed elevator.

With a shrug, Bess dashed outside.

"Isn't everything great?" she said, wide-eyed, as she stopped in front of her cousin.

"Sure is," George replied. "How's your room?"

Bess sighed cheerfully. "It's wonderful. It's—"

"I don't mean to interrupt, but do you think you could tell me later? I'm sorry, but right now I need to drop off the trailer and get Nancy's car to her. Then Pam and I are going out for coffee."

"Pam?" Bess asked, puzzled.

"My roommate," George said quickly, sticking a lighted makeup mirror under one of Bess's arms and ten or so rolled-up posters under the other. "Here, I think that's everything of yours." She opened the car door and slid behind the wheel. "Sorry to have to run. See you later," she said above the roar of the engine.

The car pulled away, then skidded to a stop. "Hey," George yelled back. "Don't forget we're meeting at Nancy's dorm for dinner tonight."

The Mustang pulled away, and Bess stood next to her suitcases on the walk, watching George turn a corner and roar off.

"No, that's all right, George," Bess muttered. "I don't want any coffee. And I'll meet Pam later. And tell you about my room later. And finish moving in—by myself."

* * *

Stumbling into her room, Nancy dropped her suitcase and let her pack slide off her shoulder.

"You must be Nancy," a cheerful voice said.

Rubbing the back of her neck, Nancy looked around for the source of the voice. A short, curvy girl with long auburn hair stood beside a bed beneath a window.

"I'm Kara," the girl said. "Since you weren't here, I started moving in. I hope you don't mind."

"I don't—" Nancy began.

Kara quickly gestured to a messy pile of clothes she was sorting through. "I took the bed by the window because I'm a little claustrophobic," she continued before Nancy could finish. "That *is* the rule of the dorm. First come, first pick." She smiled.

"That's great," Nancy said quickly, even though she was a little disappointed. It would have been nice to get the window, but it wasn't that big a deal.

"Good, I'm glad you understand," Kara said in her bubbly manner. "We'll get along great, since we know how to share. You see, I went to boarding school, and my roommate last year didn't understand the concept of sharing at all. I mean, she was incredibly selfish. I came in one day and she'd made a tape line down the middle of the room. 'Everything on this side of the line is mine,' " Kara mimicked. "That meant off limits to me. Can you believe that? What an attitude!"

Nancy felt her smile waver a little as she set

her suitcase down on the bed and opened it. "Definitely sounds unfair to me," she agreed, though secretly she hoped she wouldn't have to find out what had driven Kara's last roommate to such extremes.

"I just knew you'd understand," Kara cried. "I have a good feeling about us, Nancy, and I know I'm going to be right."

Us? Nancy wondered as she focused on her suitcase. The only *us* she'd ever considered herself half of was Ned and her. But I guess everything's different now, she realized.

She carefully lifted out the T-shirts that were folded across the top and unwrapped them. Inside were three framed pictures. Nancy began to set them up on her desk side by side.

One was a picture of her father and Hannah, their housekeeper, taken last Christmas in front of the fireplace. Another was a snapshot of her and Bess and George sitting on the hood of the Mustang just after they'd returned from visiting the Wilder campus.

"Isn't that sweet," Kara said, coming up behind her. "I brought pictures the first time I left home, too."

"It's actually not the first time I've left home—" Nancy started to explain, bringing out the third picture.

"Who's *that?*" Kara asked excitedly.

Nancy set the picture on her desk and studied it with Kara. It was her favorite picture of Ned.

He looked as if he'd just stepped out of a jeans commercial.

"He's a total hunk," Kara cried. "He isn't your boyfriend, is he?"

"Well, actually—" Nancy began.

"Wow, you are so lucky," Kara continued, cutting Nancy off. "You make the coolest couple."

"Thanks," Nancy said, surprised. She gazed wistfully at the photo and was startled by it. Even though this was the same picture she'd had on the bureau in her room in River Heights—the same one she looked at before going to sleep night after night—it just didn't seem the same. The funny thing was, as incredibly gorgeous as Ned still looked, and as familiar as his face was, he seemed strangely out of place in her new surroundings. It was as if she knew him, but didn't.

Don't be an idiot, Nancy thought, blinking her eyes to clear them. She found herself reaching for Ned's locket, then decided to leave it alone. You've known Ned for years, she reminded herself. He's still the same wonderful guy he was yesterday.

Just then Eileen came into the room. With her was a short girl with warm, burnished skin, long black hair, and a winning smile. The girl was cradling a computer keyboard in her arms.

"Hey, Nancy, this is my roomie, Reva," Eileen announced.

"Reva Ross," Reva said.

"Hi, Reva." Nancy gestured to the keyboard. "Does that belong to your computer?" she asked.

22

"Sure does." Reva smiled. "Graduation present."

"Excellent," said Nancy.

"If you need to use it . . ." Reva offered.

"Does anyone have a flashlight?" Stephanie called out from across the hall. "I lost an earring under my bureau."

"I do," volunteered Nancy, fishing her penlight out of one of the side pockets of her backpack.

"Why aren't I surprised it's you," Stephanie said, stepping into the room for Nancy's light, giving her another mocking half smile. "Were you in the Girl Scouts? You're so well-prepared."

Nancy didn't quite know what to say, but it didn't seem to matter. Stephanie wasn't waiting for an answer as she turned away and recrossed the hall.

Nancy shook her head and turned her attention to Stephanie's roommate, who had wandered in and was eyeing her stuff and Kara's. She was a thin blond girl with pale blue eyes.

"Hi," Nancy said. "I'm Nancy Drew."

"Julie Hammerman," the girl said softly. She had very pale skin, and dark half-moons under her eyes, as if she'd been studying all night or worrying. Whatever it was, it seemed as if the pressure of college was already getting to her.

She must be really nervous, Nancy guessed. What a pair. Between Stephanie's aloofness and nasty cracks, and Julie's silence, I doubt I'll be spending much time in their room.

"Anyone know if there's a soda machine

around here?" Reva asked. "I'm about to die of thirst—"

"Here's your flashlight," Stephanie called out. Nancy looked up just in time to see her penlight flying through the air toward her. She caught it in midair just before it hit her on the head.

"Always be prepared," quipped Stephanie, wagging a finger.

Something in Nancy snapped. Stephanie's rudeness had finally gotten to her. "Hey, Stephanie?" Nancy said, trying hard not to sound as annoyed as she felt. "Next time you can just say 'thanks,' okay?"

At first Stephanie acted surprised. Then she made an okay sign with her fingers and winked. "You bet."

"There's a soda machine in the basement," Eileen said, finally answering Reva's question.

Suddenly the whole suite was in Nancy's room, with everyone talking at once. Nancy was unsure if she should be smiling or grimacing at the chaos around her.

"And it's only noon," Nancy murmured to herself, glancing at her watch. "It feels like the end of the day."

She caught herself fingering her locket again and realized she reached for it every time she felt overwhelmed. Maybe, she decided, she should try to get through this first day by herself.

I have to keep reminding myself that Ned isn't here, she thought. I'm on my own. I should act that way.

Looking apologetically at Ned's picture, she reached up to her neck and undid the clasp on the locket. She laid the gold chain gently on her bureau, so it wasn't hidden, so she'd always know where it was. Then she turned back to her open suitcase.

Well, so far college wasn't exactly what she'd expected. It already looked as if there might be a few bumps in the road, she thought, glancing at Stephanie leaning casually in her doorway.

It was going to be interesting, living with so many other people. Everyone was so different.

Isn't this what you wanted, though? Nancy reminded herself as she started back down for her other suitcase and lamp. What you tried to explain to Ned and Bess—the full college experience you need to try? So now that you have it, you'd better just hope it works.

CHAPTER 2

As Bess dragged her last two suitcases off the elevator at the second floor, she could hear the bells from the campus clock tower chiming twelve for noon. She was in no mood to appreciate the melodic sound. Her shoulders were killing her, and she was still annoyed at the way George was acting toward her.

Her hallway was filled with talk and laughter. Dozens of girls with their parents in tow were shuttling around crates and trunks and electronic equipment.

At her own doorway Bess stopped short. With a look of dismay, she dropped her suitcases. Standing there with her arms full of books was the girl she'd smacked into downstairs.

She was tall and gracefully trim. Even though the day was warm, she was still wearing a kelly green sweater and chinos. Her straight brown hair was pulled tightly off her face in a ponytail.

She had big blue eyes and held her lips so tightly pressed together they could have been drawn on with a single stroke of a pencil.

She probably was pretty, Bess thought, but it would never show because she obviously hadn't smiled in years.

"You're Bess Marvin?" the girl exclaimed with unconcealed disappointment.

"Uh, yes," Bess said, smiling nervously. "And you must be Leslie—"

"King," the girl finished Bess's sentence for her.

"I'm sorry about bumping into you downstairs," Bess said. "You know, with all the confusion and every—"

"Does all this stuff really belong to you?" Leslie interrupted, waving her hands over Bess's stuff.

Her face reddening, Bess nodded, embarrassed by the heap of mismatched suitcases and one plastic garbage bag.

Leslie raised her eyebrows and surveyed the room like an inspector. "Well, I don't know where you're going to put it all," she said, turning back to arrange her books into neat rows on the shelves. Alphabetical by author, Bess noted.

Bess's heart sank. Was that all her new roommate had to say to her? Maybe she's really just shy, Bess thought.

"You're lucky to be so tall," Bess said admiringly as Leslie slid her last book onto a shelf. "And thin. I'd have to diet for a million years to look like you, but I'll bet it's no problem for you, right?"

Leslie snorted. "If you mean, do I obsess about my weight all the time, the answer is no, I don't. I have more important things on my mind."

Bess nodded, as though she understood, but she felt as if she'd been slapped in the face. Of course that wasn't what Leslie had meant, she thought.

Leslie unzipped one of her suitcases and took out a stack of underwear—all white and all folded with military precision. She carried the stack to the dresser and set it down carefully in the top drawer.

"I think we should agree on a few things right now," Leslie said over her shoulder. "That way we'll avoid misunderstandings later."

"Misunderstandings," Bess repeated dully, afraid that she knew exactly what Leslie was leading up to.

"It's a lot easier for *two people* to share *one room* if each person makes an effort *to be neat,*" Leslie said, carefully stressing the important words.

"Yes," Bess said, watching Leslie's stack of T-shirts disappear into the second drawer.

"Nothing makes a room seem smaller than a mess," Leslie continued.

"Right." Bess winced. Unfortunately, neatness was not one of her shining qualities.

"Just so you know," Leslie went on, pausing to give Bess her thin smile again, "I'm pre-med.

That means I'll be doing a lot of studying, and I plan on doing most of it right here. I'm sure we can agree that this room is not going to be party central, right?"

Bess felt herself flush. Obviously, Leslie had the wrong impression of her. Sure, she liked to have fun, but she'd never call her bedroom "party central."

"Bess?" Leslie was saying. "Do we agree?"

Bess blinked. "Sure," she said dully.

"Good." Leslie nodded with satisfaction. She went over to her dresser and started arranging bottles of shampoo and lotion from back to front, tallest to shortest.

Bess opened the first of her bags. A fuzzy pink sweater fell out.

Maybe I shouldn't put that away just yet, Bess thought, eyeing the sweater gloomily. It looks like it's going to be a chilly semester in 214 Jamison Hall.

And I thought the dorms were crazy, George said to herself that evening as she scanned the multiple food lines snaking through Thayer Hall cafeteria. The place was in an uproar with laughter and conversation. People were darting from station to station, checking out the salads, entrées, and desserts.

Actually, George was surprised at how good the food looked. Everyone who came home from college usually said the same thing: cafeteria food is evil; eat just enough to stay alive.

What planet were *they* on? George wondered, her mouth watering. Everything here looked healthy and delicious.

But where were Nancy and Bess? she wondered, scanning the tables. She was growing hungrier by the second and was just about to give up and plunge into one of the food lines, when she saw Nancy in the salad area, waving to her.

"Finally," she murmured as she headed toward the salad bar, passing tables piled with blue pamphlets from freshman orientation that afternoon. When she finally got to the salad bar, George saw Nancy eating off a plate of salad and Bess with as much food in her mouth as she had on the plate she was carrying.

"Thanks for waiting, guys." George rolled her eyes.

"Sorry, George." Nancy smiled after she swallowed. "It all just looked so good."

"It's nice to know the food won't be a problem," Bess said. "But did you hear what the dean said at the orientation about the academic rules?"

George put a hand on Bess's shoulder. Last spring, when they had all decided to go to Wilder together, George knew Bess would struggle with her courses, and that she and Nancy would have to lend a helping hand. George didn't mind, but she was a little worried for her cousin. High school classes were nothing next to what they were about to face.

"Nancy and I will help get you through, Bess," George said soothingly.

"And I'll be happy to help, too, if I can," said a deep voice from behind them.

George, Nancy, and Bess turned and found themselves staring up at a tall, very well muscled guy with blue eyes and sandy-colored hair. George thought he had great dimples, which showed because he was smiling at them. Well, at Bess, actually. George laughed to herself as Bess reddened and whirled away, embarrassed.

"You three freshmen?" he asked, directing the question to the back of Bess's head.

"How'd you guess?" George asked, waving her blue folder.

"I guess those things do sort of give you away," he admitted. "Lucky for you I don't have anything against freshmen. My name's Dave, by the way," he said, tapping Bess lightly on the shoulder. "Dave Cantera. I'm a junior. Maybe I'll see you around."

"Good job," Nancy said to Bess as they watched Dave vanish into the crowd.

"Yeah, way to leave an impression," George said. "Are you sick or something?"

"I blew it, didn't I?" Bess moaned, biting her lip.

George looked at Nancy. "Yup," she said, and laughed.

All three finished filling their plates with an assortment of salads and paid for their food. George grabbed the first three spots she saw.

There was so much noise they had to lean in just to hear one another.

"Okay," Nancy said. "Roommate report. You first, George."

"No complaints." George waved her fork in her enthusiasm. "Pam Miller. She's a jock, like me. *And* we wear the same size. I invited her to eat with us tonight, but she's thinking of joining the African-American Students Union and had to go to a party with them."

"Maybe we'll get to meet her at one of the parties later tonight," Nancy said.

"I hope so. You guys should really like her."

"What about you, Bess?" Nancy asked.

Bess jumped. "Huh? What?"

George frowned. Back at the dorm, George thought Bess had acted a little depressed, but she figured it was just a case of first-day nerves. Now she wasn't sure.

"How about you?" Nancy said again. "What's your roommate like?"

"Leslie King?" Bess smiled grimly. "She's very neat, and she's pre-med."

"Uh-oh," Nancy said.

"Five matching suitcases stacked in a perfect pyramid," Bess said, gesturing with her hands to show how they were piled just so.

"I smell trouble," George quipped.

"And"—Bess eyed them—"she folds her underwear."

George had to clamp her hand over her mouth to keep herself from losing it. But when Nancy didn't bother, George burst out laughing, too. "Oh, no! A neat-freak workaholic—and she's going to be living with Bess. Well, as they say, opposites attract. Let's hope it's true for roommates."

"I wish it were as funny as it sounds," Bess said, "but I don't think she likes me very much."

George stopped laughing and gently touched her cousin's arm. She felt bad for Bess—and more than a little guilty. Bess seemed to be off to a rocky start, and she herself couldn't be happier.

"Seriously," George said, "how could anyone dislike you, Bess? What's not to like?"

"She just doesn't know you yet, that's all," Nancy added. "Give her a few days."

"I guess," Bess said, sighing. "Otherwise, it's going to be a very long year." She put down her fork and stood. "I need something sweet to make me feel better. I'm going to see what's for dessert."

When she was gone, Nancy spoke confidentially to George. "Do you think she's okay? She seems really down."

"She'll get over it," George said. She knew her cousin. Bess never stayed depressed for long. Besides, how could anyone be sad in a place like this?

Just then George caught sight of the hunk from the food line. He was walking quickly across the dining hall. She followed his path with her eyes and saw he was making a beeline for the dessert bar, where Bess was pouring M&M's over a small hill of vanilla ice cream.

George turned away grinning to herself. A couple of minutes later Bess came hurrying back to their seats, her cheeks pink and her eyes shining. "You'll never guess."

"Wait," George said. She squeezed her eyes shut and pressed her index fingers to her temple. "I see—yes, I see a handsome man in your life," she said, imitating a fortune teller. She waved her hand over the table. "I see a big, big party."

"All right, all right," Bess said, "so his frat's having a party tonight. Zeta something. And I'm invited." She practically bubbled over. "I mean, *we*. We're all invited."

"That's great, Bess," Nancy said, beaming. "That should make up for Leslie."

"Leslie?" Bess cocked her head to one side. "Who's Leslie?"

That's the Bess I know. George smiled to herself, relieved.

"Why aren't you wearing your necklace?" George asked Nancy, eyeing the space above her blouse where Ned's locket should have been.

Nancy looked down quickly, reddened and took another stab at a cherry tomato she'd been chasing around her plate for the past few minutes. "I took it off," she said, spearing the tomato and gesturing with it offhandedly.

"Wasn't that meant to keep other guys away?" Bess asked.

"Well, I—I didn't feel like wearing it," Nancy said, trying to explain.

Nancy caught George and Bess exchange looks, but decided not to get into it with them. Even she didn't know exactly why she took it off, so why bring it up? But the fact was, she'd been reaching for the locket all through dinner. Now that she'd taken it off, she did miss it.

Maybe it was just all that confusion in my room getting on my nerves, Nancy reflected. I'll put it back on later.

"Come on up to my room," she said cheerfully, trying to change the subject. "We can get ready for the party there. And I'll introduce you to some of my suitemates."

Nancy, George, and Bess bussed their trays and hurried to the elevator. "Can I borrow your pink bodysuit, Nan?" Bess asked on the elevator to Nancy's floor. "I think you should wear that blue skirt of yours—it looks so great on you. And, George, you would be a knockout in your slip dress with the black-and-white flowers, with a black tank top underneath."

"You're amazing," Nancy replied, shaking her head. "I can't believe you know my wardrobe better than I do."

Bess buffed her nails against her sleeve. "What can I say? Some of us just have a gift."

In the lounge, Nancy introduced Bess and George to the girls who were there. Nancy did her best to keep their names straight. There was the thin, quiet blond girl named Julie who seemed so nervous and jumpy; there was a pix-ielike girl named Liz who was dressed in black from head to toe and had a faint New York accent. Stephanie was lounging on the sofa with a guy in a black leather jacket. When Nancy introduced Bess and George, Stephanie's eyes raked them over before she gave them a barely perceptible nod.

"She has a real attitude," George whispered to Nancy as they worked their way down the hallway.

"I haven't figured her out yet," Nancy admitted.

"At least you don't have to live in the same room with her," Bess said, and sighed, obviously thinking of Leslie.

"Is Leslie really as bad as—" Nancy began as she slipped her key into the lock.

As the door swung open, she froze and clamped her hand over her mouth.

"Nancy, what is it?" Bess cried.

Nancy didn't have to answer. When George and Bess rushed up behind her to peek over her shoulder, they gasped in horror.

Nancy's room was arranged like every other one in the suite, with a bed and desk and dresser for each person, and a big, floor-to-ceiling closet. But there was something distinctly different about the room now, something changed, a decorating touch that the others didn't have.

It was totally trashed.

The dresser drawers had been yanked out and

clothes spilled out from them. One of Nancy's suitcases gaped open on the floor, and more clothes lay strewn across her bed. The contents of Nancy's makeup case were scattered across her desk.

Someone had searched the room.

Someone in a hurry.

CHAPTER 3

Kara stepped off the elevator, panting from her run back to the dorm. She'd been halfway across the university's quad, on the way to a meeting, when she realized it was cooler outside than she'd thought. If she was going to go to parties later and be out late, she'd need a sweater.

When she reached the suite, Stephanie was leaning in the doorway lighting a cigarette with the smoldering end of another one.

"What, back so soon?" Stephanie inquired tonelessly, blowing a stream of smoke across Kara's face.

Kara waved the smoke away, laughing to herself. She thought Stephanie's tough girl act was just that—an act. Probably underneath all that leather and scowling was a harmless pussycat.

"I just forgot something," Kara said, brushing past her and heading down the hall to her room. She slowed when she saw two strange girls stand-

ing in her open doorway. Then her new roommate came out.

Nancy, she reminded herself. Nancy Drew.

"Hey, Nancy!" Kara said brightly. "How's it
going?"

"I'm not sure." Nancy was frowning.

Kara stopped in her tracks. "What? What is
it?"

"It looks like someone's been through our
stuff," Nancy replied.

Kara's jaw dropped with surprise. She remembered from boarding school how sometimes girls
stole things. Small stuff mostly, clothes, jewelry,
anything that could fit in a pocket. But on the
first day? Wow. That was too quick.

When Kara stuck her head in the room, she
was surprised that nothing looked different.

"Well?" she asked innocently.

Kara saw Nancy exchange surprised looks with
the two girls. She glanced at her new roommate.
"Like, what'd they get?"

Before Nancy could reply, Kara said, "By the
way—hi, I'm Kara. Nancy's roommate."

"Uh, these are my friends George and Bess,"
Nancy said. "Kara, don't you see the problem in
here? The place is totally trashed!"

"It is?" Kara said, poking her head inside
again and peeking around. She smiled. "It looks
just like it did when I left. Sorry if I made a little
mess. I was late for my meeting."

"You mean *you're* the one who left the room
like this?" Nancy asked, flabbergasted.

"So?" Kara shrugged.

"So . . ." Nancy said, pointing inside. "I don't mean to be too critical, but the room's a total wreck."

"I said I'm sorry," Kara replied, her voice heavy with disappointment. She never could understand people who had a tizzy over something as small as a little mess. Kara's own philosophy about life was: When in doubt, chill out.

"But my stuff," Nancy was saying. She waved her hand over her makeup, which was scattered all across her desk. "Wait, these things were in my—"

"Purse?" said Kara, grinning. She lifted Nancy's bag, which was tucked under her arm. "It was exactly what I needed to finish my outfit," she explained. "Anyway, didn't we agree we could share? It's not like I didn't empty it out before I took it or anything," Kara added quickly.

Kara could feel Nancy's friends glaring at her. Nancy was staring at the floor and shaking her head. Kara could tell Nancy was frustrated and wanted to say something.

"You're right, Nancy. I'm really sorry," Kara said soothingly. "I should have asked." But inside she was hoping that Nancy could relax a little more, or else it would be a long year. What was the good of living with someone if you couldn't share stuff?

Oh, well, Kara thought, if she can't deal with a little borrowing, that's her problem, not mine.

* * *

It's okay, Nancy was telling herself. Give her a chance. It's not as bad as it looks. . . .

"Listen, Kara," Nancy said, "it's okay if you borrow something, but next time, ask, all right?"

"No problemo," Kara replied, sliding past and plunging her arm into a pile of clothes. She brought out a white linen sweater and held it up like a prize fish. "It's a little chilly out there," Kara said to the girls, cutting through the tension with a thousand-watt smile.

Nancy smiled back at her roommate, though inwardly she was still annoyed. Well, it's our first day of living together, she thought, excusing her. After all, everyone makes mistakes.

"So what do you say, guys," she said, trying to smooth everything over. "Should we get ready to party?"

Before anyone could reply, Kara was waving goodbye. "I'm going to hit them all," she threw back over her shoulder.

As soon as Kara was gone, George was rolling her eyes and Bess was giggling.

"Maybe Leslie isn't so bad after all," Bess announced.

"Kara's not hopeless," Nancy said, "she's just a little, uh—"

"Much?" George threw in.

"Let's forget Kara," Nancy said, refusing to get ruffled. "Let's get ready. My makeup is—all over the place." Nancy plopped down on her bed and laughed, shaking her head at the mess.

"Face it, Nan," George said. "Kara's a slob.

Maybe you and Bess should switch roommates. You know, birds of a feather and all that."

"Thanks a lot," Bess complained.

Nancy hopped to her feet. "I refuse to make a big deal out of this. Kara'll be fine."

Nancy plunged into her closet. "Now, where's that blue skirt?" she murmured.

"And that slip dress with the flowers," George reminded her.

Nancy brought out the clothes and threw them across the bed. "Okay. We're in business. Now—where's my locket?" She searched the room with her eyes.

"Jewelry box?" George suggested.

"No," Nancy said, her mind drawing a blank. There'd been too much excitement and confusion. "I was positive I left it right on top of the bureau."

Nancy walked over to the chest of drawers and peered behind it. She leaned down and stuck her hand underneath.

"Where could it be?" she said with growing concern.

Suddenly Bess and George spoke at the same time. "Kara!" they chorused, then burst out laughing.

"I don't know." Nancy shook her head. "After all that, you'd think she would have told me if she borrowed it."

The three girls changed for the party, and retrieved the lipsticks and eye shadows scattered around the room. Nancy picked through the piles of clothes, searching for the locket. "It's hopeless trying to find anything that small in all this," she murmured.

"You'll find it," George said, slipping into Nancy's dress.

I'd better, Nancy thought to herself. Or Ned will kill me.

Finally they were ready, and Nancy led them down the narrow hall. As the door closed behind her and they entered the laughter and general chaos of the main dorm hallway, Nancy's hand went automatically to her neck and touched the bare skin at her throat where she'd promised Ned his locket would always hang. She felt a pang of regret and guilt. Not only had she lost track of his present, she hadn't even called him yet. She had promised she'd call the second she got settled. But she'd been so busy and excited, and the phone situation was so screwy, and now she and Bess and George were off to their first party as college students. . . .

I'm sure he'll understand, Nancy assured herself. I'll call him first thing in the morning.

"Let's go," Nancy cried, determined to shake off her gloom as she raced her two best friends down the hall.

Nancy squinted through the iron gates of the university's main quad, her mind racing a mile a minute, trying to take it all in. The street and sidewalk outside were full of students dancing to the music pouring out of a window. The night air was clear and crisp.

"Look, guys!" Bess said excitedly. "There it is, the Zeta house."

Nancy saw a stone mansion with turrets and towers. A flag with Greek letters fluttered limply over the door. People were pouring in and out of the huge wooden doors, and the tall windows were flashing with strobe lights. Then Nancy saw another building just like it next door. Then another. And another. As far as she could see. Fraternity row.

"Which one, Bess?" Nancy asked.

"I'm not sure," Bess replied with a mischievous smile. "I guess we'll just have to try them all."

George winked at Nancy. "So much for Dave," she whispered.

"Here we go, girls!" Bess cried, grabbing her friends and plunging into the crowd. They were swept up the steps and through the front entrance into an enormous hallway.

Nancy ran straight into the back of a huge guy. He must play football, she thought. He's probably the whole front line.

She reached up and tapped him on the shoulder. "Excuse me, is this Zeta?"

Turning around, the guy stared at Nancy, smiling stupidly.

"It is if you want it to be," he said, his speech a little slurred. He threw an arm across her shoulders.

Suddenly someone swiped the guy's hand away. "Go grab someone your own size," the new guy said. "Hi, I'm Paul," he continued after the "front line" moved on.

Paul had sandy hair and a sleek, athletic build. Much more Nancy's scale than the football player he'd just saved her from.

But why should I care? Nancy chided herself, thinking of Ned. "Nancy Drew," she said, and smiled.

"Don't worry, Nancy," Paul said. "I don't bite."

He bent forward and whispered in Nancy's ear. "Are you here with anyone?"

Nancy eyed him suspiciously.

"Don't get the wrong idea." Paul laughed good-naturedly. "You were looking around like you'd lost someone."

"I'm here with my girlfriends." When Nancy turned around to introduce Bess and George, they were gone. She craned her neck, trying to find them, but it was hopeless. "Oh, well." She shrugged. "One of my friends came looking for some guy. This is the Zeta house, isn't it?"

Paul nodded, then said, "Who's the guy?"

"I don't really know him," Nancy explained. "Some guy she met at dinner. His name is Dave."

"Dave?" Paul frowned, his laugh lines disappearing.

"Yeah. Why, what's the matter?"

"Oh, nothing. Dave's all right," he said not very convincingly. He gently led Nancy away by

45

the shoulder. "So, are you having a great time? Zeta is famous for great times."

"I guess," Nancy said.

"Come on. I'll get you some of our world-famous Zeta punch."

He does seem kind of nice, Nancy thought to herself. But if he asks me out, I'll have to tell him I have a boyfriend.

As Nancy tried to follow Paul, she got caught in a crosscurrent of traffic. By the time it passed, Paul had vanished. Nancy was alone.

Bess knew there were people who went through their entire lives without knowing the meaning of life. They were in all those incredibly long novels she'd had to read in high school English.

Bess knew the meaning of *her* life, at this moment, in this place. It was to party in college!

She'd gotten separated from Nancy and George in the crush, but she'd found Dave. Or rather, he'd found her. A hand grabbed her wrist, and when she was turned around, there he was— Dave from the cafeteria, grinning as if he'd been waiting just for her.

They began dancing in front of the frat house's candle-filled fireplace. The *thud-thud-thud* of the music worked up her feet, vibrating in her knees. She closed her eyes, bumping against the other dancers around her, moving more freely than she ever had.

Maybe it was the music, or maybe it was Dave.

The fact was, Bess didn't remember ever feeling so happy. The day had gotten off to such a lousy start, with having to move in by herself, and then finding out that Miss Uptight Neat Freak was her roommate. But all that was a million miles away now.

Dave leaned into her. He had to yell to be heard above the crashing music. "Want to get some air? Maybe I could show you around the house?"

Bess nodded and followed him through the crowd, toward the house's grand staircase. It was wide and spiraled three stories to the top floor. Dave waited for her and then led her up. The stairs were lined with couples, some talking quietly and holding hands, and a few making out hot and heavy in full view of the party below.

"Hey, Dave," one guy said, punching him playfully on the arm. "Caught one already, huh?"

Dave shot him a look that Bess didn't know how to interpret. All she knew was that the guy shut up and flattened himself against the wall. She was happy to be with someone who could make another guy back off that quickly.

"Don't listen to him," Dave said to Bess as they reached the second floor. "He's a real slob."

"So where do you guys eat?" Bess asked, trying her best to seem really interested.

"In the dining hall," Dave said. "But I can show you that later."

"What's down here?" Bess asked, peeking

through a pair of swinging doors down a long hallway.

"These," said Dave, pushing the doors open and pausing for effect, "are our bedrooms."

The doors swung shut behind them, and the party suddenly sounded far away. It was quiet enough to hear the floor creaking under their footsteps. Bess heard no sounds coming from the bedrooms. The other rooms were empty.

"The last door on the right," Dave said, leading the way.

"What's that?" Bess inquired.

"My room. What else?"

"Really?" Bess said, suddenly nervous. "I thought you were going to show me the whole house."

"Sure," Dave agreed. "That's for later, though."

"Oh," Bess muttered, trying to ignore her sudden nervousness.

Stop being a dumb high school kid, she scolded herself. Frat members have their own rooms. What's the big deal?

The last thing she wanted was for Dave to think she didn't know how to be alone with a guy.

Dave unlocked the door and pushed it open. Bess stepped in first. As Dave brushed by her to reach for the light, she felt her heart begin to beat faster and her knees start to shake, though she didn't know whether it was from giddy excitement or from anxiety.

Dave turned on a soft yellow lamp. From the way the frat house looked on the outside, she was a little disappointed with the room. It was unimpressive, just a bed and a desk and a chair, with some beer-ad posters on the wall and a plastic basketball hoop hanging limply off a door.

Still, she didn't want to be impolite. "Nice room," she said.

"Thanks," Dave replied. He leaned back against the wall and leveled a suggestive gaze at Bess. "I'm glad you like it." His mouth was still smiling, but the expression in his eyes didn't seem sweet anymore. It was leering. His eyes roamed all over her hungrily.

Bess caught her breath. Suddenly everything was happening too fast. A minute ago she was laughing and having a great time on the dance floor, and now there was nothing around her but silence and empty rooms, and some guy named Dave. And Dave's room . . .

You're in college now, she kept telling herself. You can take care of yourself. You can make your own decisions.

She leaned back against the opposite wall. She slid her hands behind her so he wouldn't see how they were shaking.

"So . . ." she began.

Then he was walking toward her. He stopped so close she could smell his breath. It smelled strongly of alcohol.

"Don't you want to talk or something?" she blurted out, sidestepping away.

"Later," said Dave, sliding with her.

She felt his hand on her elbow and closed her eyes. Then she felt his lips on hers.

She couldn't open her eyes.

You know how to kiss, so kiss, she commanded herself. She tried to pucker, but it was no good. Her lips just didn't want to do it.

Suddenly the red-and-yellow posters she'd seen tacked up all over campus flashed before her eyes. They warned about parties and drinking and what could happen. Be careful, they cautioned. Pair up with a friend and watch out for each other. Friends? What about hers? Where *were* Nancy and George? They'd be disappointed in her if they could see her now—and they'd be right. Everything those posters warned against was happening to her, or was about to happen. . . .

CHAPTER 4

"N ancy!"

Nancy whirled around at the sound of her name. Julie Hammerman was weaving toward her through the crowd, calling out her name. This Julie wasn't the pale, frightened girl Nancy had met that afternoon. That Julie had gone through a total transformation: her thin blond hair was now tousled and wild, her eyes electrically alive. She was grinning from ear to ear and wearing a clingy, little black dress. In one hand she gripped an empty cup. Her other arm was wrapped around a guy.

"I've been looking *all* over for you," Julie said.

"You have?" Nancy said.

"This is Frank—I mean Stew—"

"Todd," the guy corrected with a grin.

Julie leaned forward conspiratorially. "Isn't this awesome!"

"I guess it is," Nancy said, laughing. Boy, Julie

seems to have come out of her shell, she thought. "I'm glad to see you've cheered up."

"Oh, don't worry about me," Julie said, waving her cup dismissively. "I'm just a little moody." She started hopping up and down. "Hey, let's dance. Wanna dance, Stew?"

"Todd," the guy repeated, shaking his head.

"Julie?" someone cut in. "How utterly amusing! My harmless little roomie chatting with Junior Miss America."

Nancy knew who it was without turning around.

"Hi, Stephanie." Julie grinned, unfazed by her roommate's sarcastic comment.

Stephanie was wearing a black bodysuit that looked as though it had been painted on. With her brown lipstick and black hair, her exotic face was even more mysterious.

"What, empty-handed?" Stephanie remarked, nodding at Nancy. "Julie, why don't you send your big strong friend here over to the table to get Nancy something to hold on to."

"That's okay," Nancy said. "I'll pass."

"Oh, that's right," Stephanie said cruelly. "I forgot, the Girl Scout. Always prepared—always in control."

Stephanie started to laugh. Julie seemed unsure what to do and giggled nervously. Nancy smiled slightly.

"Have you taken a good inventory of your personal stuff?" Stephanie asked.

Immediately Nancy's guard went up, thinking

she was about to be the butt of one of Stephanie's verbal traps. "I didn't know I had to," she said coolly. "Why?"

"Oh, no reason—" Stephanie said.

"Some of her money's missing," Julie whispered loudly.

"Julie!" Stephanie rolled her eyes. "I told you I didn't want to make a federal case about it."

"I'm sorry to hear it," Nancy said, but inside, she couldn't help thinking that it couldn't have happened to a better person.

"No big deal," Stephanie replied, leading Julie away by the hand. "Let's leave Nancy to—well, whatever it was she was doing. Don't stay out late now, Nancy," she said, wagging her finger.

What is her problem? Nancy wondered, annoyed. She watched Stephanie slink away through the crowd. Then she remembered her missing locket and put it together with Stephanie's missing money. She started to wonder. . . .

Thinking about the locket shifted her attention to Ned. What was he doing right then? He'd said he might try to get a jump on some of his classes this weekend. He had a hard semester ahead of him.

Suddenly a plastic cup appeared in front of her. "Nancy, there you are! I thought I'd lost you."

"Oh, Paul," Nancy said with enthusiasm.

"Hey, I was thinking, how about going for a walk or something with me? I'm busy tomorrow, but I could give you a grand tour of the campus on Monday."

"I've had a tour of the campus already," Nancy replied. "Last spring."

"But I'll show you the real Wilder, the things they don't show on school tours, the things they don't want you to see."

"Oh, *will* you," Nancy said, eyeing him skeptically.

"I know what you're thinking." Paul laughed good-naturedly. "But I really mean it. You just seem—I don't know—nice, different."

"Paul, I think you should know I have a boyfriend," Nancy said.

"I figured as much," Paul replied easily. "To tell you the truth, I would have been surprised if you hadn't. But does that mean you can't even talk to me? You're worried I'm going to steal you away, right?"

Nancy just smiled.

"Look, it's no big deal or anything," Paul said. "Just an hour's walk around school. You tell me about you. I tell you about me. Then I'll let you go. Promise."

It does sound harmless, Nancy thought. And he seems like a really nice guy.

"Okay, you're on," she replied.

"Excellent. How's two o'clock? I'll pick you up outside your dorm. Which one is it?"

"Thayer."

"Thayer it is."

As Nancy watched him plunge back into the crowd, she felt a little jump in her heart rate. But was it excitement—or guilt?

Way to go, Nancy, she thought, Ned's probably in the Emerson library right now, slaving over his books, and you're here partying the night away, meeting other guys. You've already lost his locket, and you haven't even called him yet. . . .

Paul turned around and waved back through the crowd.

"See you Monday!" he called.

"Right," Nancy whispered uncertainly, confused. "See you Monday."

Bess knew there was no one to help her. The floor was empty. There were five hundred people in this frat house, but they were all downstairs partying. They'd never hear her if she called for help.

"Hey," she said, pushing Dave's hand off her shoulder.

"What's the matter?" he said, fingering the edge of her sleeve. "Haven't I told you how beautiful you are?"

"All right, that's enough," Bess said, taking Dave's hand and pushing it away again. She tried to step to the side, but her legs were wobbly and she fell right into Dave's arms.

"Now, that's more like it," he said with slurred speech.

Bess, she said to herself, this guy is totally drunk. And you're a complete idiot.

"Dave," she said, almost yelling now. "I don't want to do this!"

"But I do."

"No!" Bess screamed, but she knew there was no one to hear her.

It was like swimming against the current, with Dave pulling her back and her fatigue pushing her down, but finally she forced her way out of Dave's hands. She was free, out of breath, and stumbling across the room for the door.

When she realized Dave wasn't coming after her, Bess paused in the open doorway. She glared at him. He was leaning against his desk, his shirt half unbuttoned, one shoe off, his eyes fluttering closed. He wasn't the cool upperclassman she'd met in the cafeteria a few hours earlier.

"You're a jerk," she blurted out, surprised at herself for speaking.

"At least I mean what I say," Dave said, unruffled. "At least I'm no tease."

"Tease? What are you talking about?"

Dave laughed ruefully. "Come on, Betty—"

"Bess!" she shouted at him.

"You knew why I invited you to the party," Dave said suggestively.

"Because I thought you liked me," she said angrily.

"Come on," Dave countered with a cruel smile. "That innocent act doesn't work with me. I've seen too many girls at this college turn it on and off. Not even ditzy little freshmen are that clueless."

Bess crossed her arms protectively over her chest. "What am I to you, just a piece of meat?

It doesn't even matter what my name is. Betty, Bess—"

Dave shrugged and sat down heavily in his chair.

Bess was boiling over with anger and confusion. She wanted to say something perfectly fitting, something this jerk would never forget—if only she knew what it was.

Knowing she was on the verge of tears, she bit her lower lip and swallowed hard. She wasn't going to give this creep the satisfaction.

She turned and ran, sprinting full tilt down the hall and through the double doors. She took the steps two at a time and pushed through the crowds of dancing and laughing students. Finally she was out in the cool night air.

Still running—she needed to run—Bess made it across the quad, flying by the classroom buildings. She stopped beneath a tree and, doubled over, heaving for breath. Tears were streaming down her face; she tasted their salty wetness on her lips. Then she heard them—her own soft sobs.

Welcome to college, a voice pounded, you made it. Have a great four years. . . .

"Nancy?" she whimpered into the darkness. "George? Where are you?"

CHAPTER 5

The next morning, Stephanie opened one eye, shielding it with her pillow from the sunlight slicing through the blinds. She looked at the alarm clock and grimaced. She was used to sleeping until noon. It was only eight, practically dawn!

Outside the window, birds were singing.

"It's disgusting," Stephanie muttered, picking a shoe off the floor and throwing it against the window, scaring the birds off. "A girl can't get any peace around here."

She reached out to her nightstand for her cigarettes, lit one, and blew smoke rings over to Julie's side of the room. Julie wasn't moving. Stephanie eyed her curiously. She had to admit, even she couldn't figure Julie out: one second the girl was a sniveling little brat, the next she was deliciously mean.

She's like a candle flame, Stephanie thought to herself. Up and down in the breeze.

"Oh, well, she owes me one," Stephanie purred, picturing the scene the night before, when she had to carry Julie home. One minute she was dancing, then all at once Julie collapsed like a rag doll right into her arms.

"Yes," Stephanie said, admiring the high-security padlock she'd bolted onto the bottom drawer of her bureau, "She definitely owes me big-time."

"Boy, am I starving," Nancy murmured, sitting up in bed.

At first she didn't know where she was. Her clear blue eyes took in the room and paused on the strange, sleeping girl in the bed against the opposite wall. Then she saw the messy piles of clothes. All at once Nancy remembered and smiled. Wilder University—Thayer Hall—Kara . . . she recalled in that order.

She pulled on her blue jeans and a T-shirt as quietly as she could. Kara seemed the type to sleep through a convoy of army trucks rumbling by her bed. Still, Nancy slipped silently out of the room, trying to be as considerate as possible on their first morning as roommates.

After the hordes of hungry freshmen in the food lines the night before, the cafeteria seemed practically deserted for breakfast. Just a few groups of chatty girls and a couple of students lazily pushing brooms. Nancy figured that this was the typical Sunday morning breakfast crowd, with most everybody sleeping in, recuperating from Saturday night parties.

Her stomach gave a plaintive rumble as she stepped up to the griddle station display case: omelettes and home fries, bacon and pancakes.

"Yogurt and granola," Nancy reminded herself, trying to be healthy.

She took her bowl to a table behind a group of girls she recognized from another suite on her floor. She smiled at the one or two she'd actually met, but they were too engrossed in conversation to notice. Nancy started to eat, but what she heard made her stop and listen.

"And get this," one girl with a black crew cut and a ring through her nose said casually, "the ambulance pulled right up to Zeta, in front of all those people. And she started screaming at the top of her lungs, swinging at the paramedics until they had to strap her arms and legs to the stretcher."

"I heard she passed out right in the hall," another said.

"Does anybody know who she is?" someone else asked.

"They're not saying," the black-haired girl replied. "Only that she was a freshman."

"Boy, I hope it's no one I know," the second girl said.

"It's all hush-hush so far," the first girl continued, waiting a beat before going on. "The administration isn't saying who it was, or what it was. But I heard that she's in the hospital and had to have her stomach pumped."

The table fell silent for a second.

It must have happened after I left the party, Nancy thought to herself.

"Maybe it was something she ate," a small, quiet girl chimed in earnestly, drawing snickers from the rest of the table.

"All I know is, I never heard of anyone eating or dancing themselves to the hospital," the black-haired girl replied.

Nancy stared down at her food and made an unenthusiastic pass at it with her spoon before giving up. She bussed her tray and walked slowly back up to her room, sobered by the thought of someone having an experience like that on her first night at college.

When she got back to the suite and opened the door to her room, what she found made all her dark thoughts disappear.

The curtains were thrown back, the windows were open to the cool morning air. Not only was Kara awake, but she was dressed for serious cleaning—jeans and a gray sweatshirt with the sleeves pushed up to the elbows. She was a whirl of activity: her sea green eyes sparkling and her long hair tied back off her face. And was that really a pile of clothes in her arms?

" 'Morning, early bird," Kara said, blowing a rebellious strand out of her eyes.

Nancy peered around the room, astonished. Kara's bed was made, and her numerous little piles of debris were now one big pile. It was actually Nancy's side that seemed a little messy now.

"Here, let me clean up my stuff," Nancy said, running over to her bed and quickly making it.

"I didn't know you were such an early riser," Kara said distractedly, picking at her pile of clothes with determination. "Then again, if I thought about it, I probably would have guessed you were the type. Silly me."

Kara impulsively dropped her armful of clothes and hopped up onto her desk to arrange some knickknacks on her top shelf. Nancy followed Kara's example by starting to put away the rest of her stuff.

"I'm sorry I didn't wait for you before going to breakfast," Nancy explained, "but you looked so sound asleep."

"It's me who should be apologizing," Kara said over her shoulder. "I thought a lot about what happened last night, and you don't have to worry, I won't take anything without asking again."

"It wasn't that big a deal—" Nancy started to say.

"No, no, you were right," Kara insisted, springing down from her desk and making another go at her clothes. "I left your bag on your desk," Kara continued. "I cleaned it out and everything."

"I really didn't mean to complain so much about that stupid little purse," Nancy said.

"Really? Well, now that you put it that way," Kara began slyly, "about that little red dress in your closet—"

Nancy shot her a guarded look.

Kara smiled broadly, her eyes flashing. "Just kidding."

Nancy breathed with relief. "No hard feelings?"

"About what?" Kara said airily, as though she'd already forgotten.

Something about the way Kara smiled told Nancy that she hadn't forgotten anything, though. Which reminded her . . .

Her blue eyes rested on the top of her bureau, where she'd left Ned's locket. "By the way, you didn't happen to see my gold locket, did you?"

"What do you mean?" Kara asked.

"I don't know. I couldn't find it last night, and I remember taking it off. I'm pretty sure I left it on top of my bureau."

Kara stiffened and folded her arms over her chest. "Lockets aren't my style," she said.

"I didn't mean you took it," Nancy replied quickly. "I thought maybe—"

"I borrowed it?" Kara said.

Nancy was embarrassed, but still, she had to ask. "Well—did you?"

Kara got up and stood in front of her dresser with her back to Nancy, loudly snapping her drawers open and closed, pretending to straighten her things. "I can't believe you'd think I'd take your locket," she said, shaking her head. Suddenly she froze. "Hey, wait a second," she cried. "It's gone!"

"What's gone?" said Nancy.

Kara whirled around, her eyes scanning the

room. "My charm bracelet. I put it in the top drawer of my dresser under a T-shirt, and now it's not there!"

"Are you sure it didn't get sucked up in Tornado Kara?" Nancy asked.

"No, I'm totally sure," Kara insisted. "I remember exactly. I put it right under that T-shirt. It was the first thing I did after I brought up my stuff."

Nancy nodded. She believed her. It was a strange coincidence that both of them were missing jewelry. Strange—or unlikely? Could they have both misplaced the one thing that meant the most to each of them? And what about Stephanie's money?

Just then there was a knock on the door. Both Nancy and Kara were startled.

"Nan, are you there?"

"Bess?" Nancy said, jumping to open the door.

The last Nancy had seen of Bess was early on at the Zeta party. Bess had been dancing with Dave, laughing and glowing with pleasure. Nancy thought she'd never seen Bess so happy and relaxed, and she didn't have the heart to interrupt just to say goodbye.

The Bess who stood there now was a far cry from the Bess she'd left at the Zeta house. Her hair was tangled, and she had puffy red pouches under her eyes, as if she'd been up all night.

And she wasn't smiling.

"So, how does Intro to the Human Brain sound?" George wondered out loud, taking the pencil from behind her ear and circling Psych 101.

"Sounds like this, 'George Fayne, I'd like to introduce you to the Brain. Mr. Brain, meet George Fayne.'" Pam Miller smiled as she leaned over to read the course description.

George couldn't help but laugh.

"Well, does that mean you don't think it would be a very challenging class?" George asked.

"I don't know," Pam admitted. "It sounds interesting, but as a rule, intro classes are pretty sketchy. Unless you're interested in the field. Then it's worth taking this class now so you can take the higher level classes later."

George nodded as she continued to pore over the catalog, trying to piece together the best class schedule for her first semester.

The weather was warm, and the sun-dappled grass on the quad where they were sitting was littered with students dozing, laughing, or browsing through course catalogs. The air was filled with rock music blaring out from the houses on Fraternity Row.

Just like a movie, George thought, smiling so hard her cheeks were beginning to ache. She didn't think she could be much happier than this: college was everything she'd hoped it would be.

And her roommate was even better.

George thought Pam Miller was perfect. Cheerful, smart, and ambitious enough to take everything seriously, but not so serious that she was going to let anything stand between her and a good time.

The night before, they'd both returned from parties at the same time and stayed up until four, sitting cross-legged on their beds, telling each other all about themselves. It was amazing how close they had become in those few hours. George felt as if she'd known Pam for years.

They decided to spend the morning together on the quad, helping each other decide what classes to register for on Monday morning.

As George flipped through the pages of the catalog, a long white envelope fell out.

"What's this?" Pam asked, picking the envelope up out of the grass.

"I don't know what it is. It was waiting for me in my mailbox this morning."

"Return address: U.S. Government," Pam said, then squinted at George. "You're not an undercover agent for the CIA or anything, are you?"

George snorted, and Pam dropped the letter when something in the catalog caught her eye.

"How about Geology 101?" she threw out.

"Rocks for jocks?" George said dubiously.

"You're right," Pam agreed. "Too easy."

"Hey, look at this," George said, pointing at her course catalog.

"Hey, look at *that*," Pam countered.

George followed Pam's gaze toward a pair of well-tanned hunks jogging across the quad.

George laughed to herself, glad that even though Pam was sexy and athletic, and obviously in no need of extra attention from guys, she didn't think it was beneath her to scope out the male territory.

"Hey," Pam said, craning her neck and peering over George's shoulder. "Remember that guy you told me about from the party last night?"

"Which one? Harry Thistlewaite the Third, or the gorgeous guy I didn't have the nerve to speak to?"

"Mr. Gorgeous," Pam said, fanning herself with the single piece of mail George had retrieved from her box that morning. "Isn't that him?"

George let the catalog pages fan themselves shut as she raised her hand to shield her eyes from the sun. A tall, striking-looking guy with thick straight-black hair was strolling toward them, carrying his shirt in his hand. His body was lean and well-defined, and his coppery skin glowed in the sun. His walk was smooth and fluid, with no wasted motion.

"That's the guy," George said, hiding her face in her catalog.

Pam nodded. "I thought so, after the detailed description you gave me. There's definitely no one else around here who looks like him."

George had to agree. There might be twenty thousand students on campus, but there was no mistaking that face. The party wasn't the first time George had seen him, either. She'd noticed him at dinner in the dining hall and thought he was one of the most unusual and handsome guys she'd ever seen, with his black hair, high cheek-bones, and almond-shaped eyes. When she bussed her tray, she overheard him discussing the university's new hiring policies for minority professors. He'd sounded passionate and articulate.

"Hey, George!" Pam whispered. "He's looking this way."

George peeked over the top of her course catalog, almost afraid to see if it was true. But Pam was right. He was smiling at them. Wait. Not at *them,* but at *her.*

"Ooh," Pam said, openly watching him turn and head for Java Joe's, the campus coffee bar.

Pam looked at George and, laughing, started fanning her with the government letter. "It's a good thing the sun's out, so no one can tell whether you're blushing or catching a burn."

Embarrassed by her reaction, George wanted to change the subject. Her eyes fell on the letter. "What *is* that, anyway?" she asked.

Pam tore at the envelope. "May I?" she asked as she was peeling back the paper.

"You already have," George said, laughing.

" 'The United States government requires all males to register with the Selective Service at a local post office on or soon after their eighteenth birthday,' " Pam read.

"That's nice," George said. "So what do they want from me, applause?"

Pam read the rest to herself. At first she started giggling. Then she moaned, "Uh-oh," then an

"Oh, boy." Finally she cut loose in all-out hysterics.

"What?" George cried, sitting up.

Pam was laughing so hard she couldn't speak, and George had to snatch the letter away and read it for herself.

" 'Our records indicate that you, George Fayne, have failed to so register,' " George read aloud. " 'Failure to register for the Selective Service is a federal crime punishable by heavy fine and/or prison sentence—' "

George shook her head in confusion. "What is this, a joke? I don't get it."

"I'll have to find myself a new roommate." Pam snickered. "It seems as if you're going to be spending some time behind bars."

"It's not funny, Pam," George protested, trying unsuccessfully not to laugh. Shaking her head at the letter in disbelief, she said, "The government thinks I'm a guy!"

"Bess, are you okay?" Nancy asked, pulling her friend into the room.

"Sure, why do you ask?" Bess smiled bravely, but the attempt failed. Frowning, she looked on the verge of tears.

"Because you're obviously very upset, that's why," Nancy said.

Bess sat down heavily on Nancy's bed, her eyes filled with tears.

"How was Dave?" Nancy asked, sitting next to her friend. "Did you guys have a good time?"

Bess didn't say a thing.

Nancy touched Bess's knee. "You want to tell me about it?" she prodded gently.

Just as Bess looked as if she was getting ready to speak, there was another knock on the door.

"Want me to get that?" Kara asked from the other side of the room.

"Thanks," Nancy said.

When Kara opened the door, Julie Hammerman stuck her head inside. She kept her eyes on the floor.

"Uh, Nancy—I'm really, really sorry to bother you. . . ." she began.

"What is it, Julie?"

"There's a—well, I guess—the phone out here's for you."

"For me?" Nancy asked, surprised. It was her first phone call in college, and for a second she forgot that she could receive calls on their suite phone. "Who is it? I don't think anyone even knows the number. Come to think of it, *I* don't even know the number."

"It's a—well, I think it's a guy," said Julie, then disappeared.

"It's Ned," Bess whispered hoarsely, still staring off into space.

"It is?" Nancy cocked an eye at her. "But how do you know?"

"Who else would bother to track you down?" Bess rationalized.

Nancy could feel her heart beat faster at the thought of talking to Ned. She'd forgotten to call him—again. Unconsciously, something had been keeping her from making that call. And every hour she didn't call was another hour to explain, another hour to excuse. Was it just because she lost his locket, or was it something else—something more?

"Um, Nancy?" Julie said, poking in her head again. "I'm really sorry, but he's still there. He says it's kind of important."

"Okay, okay," said Nancy. She turned to Bess, who looked as though she needed her attention more than Ned did. Maybe talking to Bess would be easier. Then again, why put off the inevitable?

"Sorry, Bess," she said, "I'll make this really quick, so we can talk, okay?"

As she went to the phone in the lounge, Nancy tried to prepare a good reason for her silence. She realized she didn't have one.

"Hello, Ned?" she said hesitantly.

"Nancy!" Ned cried. "I'm glad I finally tracked you down."

"Ned, I'm so sorry—"

"You said you'd call me yesterday."

"I know, I know." Nancy winced. "Look, things are kind of chaotic here, and Bess is waiting in my room, and she looks kind of—"

"I was waiting for your call," Ned interrupted, "and then I spent all morning convincing some half-asleep operator at the switchboard to give me your number. I *miss* you," Ned whispered lovingly.

Nancy felt a shift in her heart. So she had nothing to fear after all. She wanted to tell him she loved him and still needed him. But the suite's lounge was nowhere to be trading sweet nothings—girls were in and out all the time.

"Ned, it's so crazy here," she said.

"Do you miss me?"

Nancy cupped her hand over the phone. "Of course I miss you," she said.

But as luck would have it, Stephanie just had to be walking by at that exact moment. Nancy rolled her eyes. She found it impossible to reassure Ned through a telephone receiver, especially when the whole world was listening. "Come on, Ned, don't you remember what it's like the first few days of college?"

"Sure, I remember," he said, unable to conceal the disappointment in his voice. "I remember I called you four times in the first two days."

"Oh, Ned—"

"And, I sent a bouquet of flowers to you, and I drove down to see you every free weekend I had."

Of course, he was right, Nancy realized. Maybe she'd just been using all the commotion here as an excuse.

"I just knew you shouldn't have gone to Wilder," Nancy heard Ned mutter under his breath.

Suddenly something in Nancy's stomach dropped, like a bowling ball off a shelf. She had always thought of them as equal partners, and the decision to go to Wilder had been hers alone. Even though Ned hadn't jumped for joy over it,

Nancy had believed he'd accepted it. Now she heard something else in his voice. He'd been jealous before, but this sounded different.

"You know what I mean," Ned tried to explain, obviously sensing the chill in Nancy's silence.

"Not really," she said firmly. "But frankly, this isn't the time to discuss it."

"Well, when *is* a good time?" Ned demanded.

"Later," Nancy said, not eager to please him. "I'll call you later, okay? I promise."

Just as she put down the phone, she realized that she'd forgotten to tell Ned about her planned walk with Paul. She'd decided to tell Ned right away, just so there wouldn't be any misunderstandings or mixed messages later on. Probably just as well, Nancy realized. He hadn't seemed in the mood for that piece of news.

"I'm sorry, Bess," Nancy began as she walked back into her room. There was no need for an apology because there was no one to accept it. The only sign that anyone had been there were the creases in Nancy's bedspread where Bess had been sitting. Her friend was gone.

CHAPTER 6

The aroma of cappuccino reached Nancy even before she stepped through the door of Java Joe's. Even though it was late Sunday afternoon, the place was packed. Nancy figured that everyone was taking advantage of the few days of freedom left before they had to hit the books.

She joined the end of the food line, craning her neck to find two of her new suitemates, Ginny Yuen and Liz Bader. They shared the room next door to hers and Kara's. Nancy figured that since they'd be sharing a wall for the next year, it would be a good idea to get to know them over a cup of coffee.

Nancy ordered an iced cappuccino and a bran muffin and stood on her toes, scanning the room. Inwardly, though, she was preoccupied. She'd been worried about Bess ever since their conversation had been interrupted by Ned's call. Bess had been really troubled about something, and

Nancy had been trying to catch up with her all day to find out what was wrong and to offer her help or support. But Bess wasn't in her room any of the three times Nancy had stopped by.

"Nancy, over here!" she heard over the din.

Nancy turned and spotted Ginny and Liz in a booth against the far wall. As she made her way toward them, twisting and turning around the little café tables crammed with students, she noticed that once again Liz was wearing nothing but black. It's what everyone wore in New York City, which was where she lived, she'd told Nancy. Ginny was wearing an aquamarine T-shirt, accentuating the ivory of her skin and the jet black of her long straight hair.

It doesn't look as if they'll ever run into problems about sharing each other's clothes, Nancy couldn't help thinking a little jealously.

Nancy slid in opposite them. "Hey, there," she said, temporarily willing away her worries about Bess. "How's everything?"

"Well, actually—" Liz began.

"Everything was fine," Ginny said, her eyes flashing in anger. "Until this morning."

"What do you mean?" Nancy asked, suddenly concerned.

"Someone broke into our room last night—" Liz explained.

"And took all of my money," Ginny finished.

"That's terrible!" Nancy said, sinking against the back of the booth in disappointed surprise. These disappearances in the suite were getting too weird. She wanted to tell them about the other missing things, then thought better of it. After all, why start a panic? Maybe it was all just a coincidence.

"Do you mind my asking how much money was taken?" she asked.

"A lot to me," Ginny said stiffly. "Everything I'd saved for books and supplies for the whole semester. I don't have anything left. Liz even had to pay for my coffee," Ginny muttered, clenching her jaw.

"I told you I didn't mind," Liz said. "I'll help you any way I can. Unfortunately, we're more used to this where I come from."

Ginny nodded. "I know you'll help. And I appreciate it. But I'm *not* used to it. I *don't* like feeling helpless, and I *don't* like feeling stupid. I just shouldn't have had all that cash on me."

"Did you report it?" Nancy asked.

"We told the floor resident advisor," replied Liz.

"The R.A.? Her name's Dawn, right?" asked Nancy.

Liz and Ginny nodded together. "Yeah, Dawn Steiger," Ginny explained. "She was really cool about it. She said she'd report it to the campus police."

"But she also said that money was impossible to trace," Liz added. "Unlike jewelry and stuff. So we shouldn't get our hopes up."

Jewelry, Nancy thought, picturing her gold locket. Something about this was bugging her.

She always relied on her sixth sense, and her sixth sense was feeling trouble.

"So," Nancy began casually, not wanting to sound too much like a detective, "when did you first notice the money was gone?"

"When Liz and I came back from the parties last night. You saw us, Nancy, we rode the elevator up together, when was it?"

"About eleven-thirty," Nancy murmured, making a mental note. "Where was the money hidden?"

"Since we just moved in, I didn't have time to find a good hiding place," Ginny began. "I figured I'd spend most of it in the next few days on books and supplies, so I just stuck it in a sock in a dresser drawer. I had no idea I had to be so careful—" Ginny stopped abruptly and shrugged.

"It's okay," Liz said, putting an arm around her roommate's shoulders.

"You'll get your money back," Nancy said assuredly.

"What can she do about it now?" Liz asked.

"I'll call my parents," Ginny decided. "Maybe they can wire me more money."

"Talk to someone in the dean's office," Nancy suggested. "They might let you buy everything you need on credit."

"Do you think they'd really do that?" Liz asked doubtfully.

"I've got to find a way to buy my books," Ginny said.

"Hey, you can have mine if you want them so badly," Liz joked.

"Thanks a lot, roomie." Ginny smiled back.

Nancy was thinking about what Ginny had said. "After you saw the money was missing, did you notice anything different about the room?" she asked.

Ginny and Liz looked at each other and shrugged. "Like what?" Liz asked.

"Drawers pulled out, clothes thrown on the floor, something different from the way you left it."

"Not really," Liz said.

"Wait a minute," Ginny said. "There *was* something. I'd been making notes about what classes I might sign up for. I left them stacked on my desk. When I got back I thought they looked sort of shuffled around."

"Like someone was reading them?" Nancy asked.

Ginny nodded. "I'd forgotten all about that. But why would a thief risk getting caught by wasting time with my notes about classes?"

"Registration is on Monday," Nancy mused. "Maybe whoever it was is interested in one of the classes you're taking and wanted to read the notes you wrote about the class." Nancy looked at Ginny and Liz. "Whoever took your money felt comfortable enough in your room to spend time looking through your socks."

"You mean you think it was someone we

know?" Ginny asked, quickly picking up on Nancy's train of thought.

"Maybe," Nancy admitted carefully. "Sometimes, when something of yours is ripped off, the thief is someone you'd never suspect, even someone you're close to."

Liz shook her head. "Don't you think whoever it was would be more worried about getting caught?"

"Not if the thief knew exactly how much time he or she had," Nancy thought out loud. She pictured the crowds at the frat parties, chatting and laughing and dancing. As far as she remembered, she'd run into just about everyone from their suite. But there were so many people, it would have been simple to "get lost" for a while and return without being noticed.

The girls sat in silence for a moment. Ginny turned and squinted at Liz as if she were accusing her.

"Hey, don't look at me!" Liz joked, shaking her head. "I was with you every second last night."

Ginny wagged her finger. "But you *did* go to the bathroom unattended—a *number* of times, if I remember," she said, then erupted in laughter.

Even though Nancy was laughing with the others, she was worried. The fact was, if these disappearances kept up, the friendliness in the suite would vanish. She had seen situations like this before: someone would point the finger at someone else, and the accusations would start to fly.

Friends, and even roommates, might end up as enemies.

"You know, Nancy," Liz joked, breaking Nancy out of her reverie. "It sounds like you've done this before."

"What do you mean?" Nancy asked defensively.

"Just the way you gave us the third degree," she said.

"Yeah, you sound like a private detective, or something," Ginny added.

"Well, my father's a criminal lawyer," Nancy explained quickly. "He knows everything about the law, and just living with him, I guess some of it rubbed off."

"I'll say," Liz said. "Do you want to be a lawyer?"

"Yeah, you seem to have the talent for it," Ginny added.

Nancy only shrugged. Smiling shyly, she was gazing out the window at the beautiful day outside. But she didn't see a thing. She was distracted by the sudden pang of regret that she'd opened her mouth at all.

When she'd decided to go to college, she'd made a decision to focus her energies on pursuing a degree in journalism and enjoying college life. Getting involved in a mystery would only separate her from her new friends. She didn't want to be on the lookout all the time. She didn't want to be suspicious of everyone.

If I get into this, she thought, won't I be risking

everything I want? The normal friendships I'm trying to build? My new life as a regular college student?

"So what do you think?" Ginny leaned across the table and spoke, breaking into Nancy's thoughts.

Nancy sipped her iced cappuccino.

"I'm not sure what to think," Nancy replied, hiding behind her cup as she finished the thought to herself. *I'm still trying to figure out if I'm just a normal college freshman.*

Early that evening Nancy's suitemates were draped over the chairs and couches in the lounge, hanging out and talking excitedly about the room-to-room party on the second floor of Thayer later that night.

"Thank goodness we've got all-guy floors here," Eileen said.

"So does that mean we stay in our rooms?" Kara asked.

"No, it's the *guys'* party," Liz explained. "We're their guests. Our job is to mingle."

"Good thing we cleaned up today, hey, roomie?" Kara winked at Nancy. "What about you, Julie, you psyched, or what?"

Julie was sitting on the floor, staring blankly at the opposite wall. She didn't respond.

"Julie?" Kara said again.

"Julie, dear!" Stephanie barked at her roommate. "The masses are calling your name!"

"Wh-what?" Julie said, sounding as if she had

a mouthful of cotton. She looked sluggishly around the room, her eyes slightly bloodshot.

"Partied a little too hard last night, did we?" Nancy asked.

"Oh, let her dry out." Stephanie waved her hand, unfolding her lean body over the couch. "You all go and mingle. I'll entertain anyone who drops by."

"Or lock us all out," Liz muttered.

"This party is open to people outside the dorm, isn't it?" Nancy asked, thinking of George and Bess.

"Oh, I don't know," Stephanie cried with mock horror. "Maybe we should get passes from the hall monitor."

Nancy smiled despite herself, trying to shake off the edgy mood Stephanie always put her in.

She was about to leave to find Bess and George so that she could invite them, when Reva came out of her room. She was Eileen's roommate, the one with the new computer. Nancy had talked to her only briefly. But what Nancy hadn't realized until now was how beautiful Reva was.

The day before, as she'd introduced herself around the suite, Reva had looked energetically alive and happy. Now she wore a dark, puzzled look on her face. Her eyes were wet, as if she were near tears. In the palm of her hand was a small, black velvet bag, the kind fancy jewelry came in. Everyone could see that it was empty.

"Did anyone see a really old pocket watch lying around?" Reva asked, more as a plea than a question. "It was silver," she continued, when no one spoke up, "and had engraved flowers around the edges. It was a family heirloom, my great-grandfather's—"

"Funny you should mention it," Eileen chimed in. "Because I haven't been able to find my jade ring. My old boyfriend brought it back for me from Morocco."

"Bummer," Julie mumbled, nodding sadly.

Suddenly everyone started talking at once about some thing that was missing.

"Hey, didn't I see you snooping around my room last night?" Reva challenged Liz.

"I was only checking to see if you had any lipstick I could borrow," Liz explained resentfully.

"How do I know you're telling the truth?" Reva said, her hands on her hips.

"Because she *is,* that's how," Ginny said, stepping in, coming to the defense of her roommate. "Liz would never steal anything. I had a lot of cash stolen, and Liz was the first one to help me out, unlike the rest of you—"

Nancy saw Reva throw Liz a glance that might have been suspicious and might not. Liz, insulted, turned her back and stalked out to her room.

Nancy's mind was racing a mile a minute. How could she stay out of this mess any longer? Her worst predictions were coming true. In under a minute the atmosphere in the suite had become horribly strained. One more muttered accusation, one more suspicious look, and friendships in the suite would be ruined for the year.

Okay, Nancy, she commanded herself. Start thinking.

Whoever the thief is, is really good. Efficient, fast, striking quickly to take something small, something whose absence won't be noticed right away. And there are no obvious suspects. Everyone has lost something. Then again, a thief's most common tactic is to cry thief herself, to deflect suspicion from herself.

It could be anyone in the suite, Nancy realized. Or it could have been no one.

"Yawn." Stephanie patted her mouth as she stood up from the couch. "This little gathering is *so* stimulating, I just can't tear myself away."

"Oh, sorry, Stephanie," Reva remarked acidly. "We didn't mean to detain you."

"Quite all right," Stephanie quipped, and started down the hall.

"But didn't you lose something, too, Stephanie?" Nancy called after her.

Stephanie turned partway around. "What? Me?"

"I thought you said some of your money was missing," Nancy prodded.

"I did?" Stephanie acted surprised. "Oh, that. Just some cash. But that's life. Easy come, easy go," she said with a wave, and closed her door behind her.

The group broke up in moody silence, all the girls acting frustrated and depressed as they went to their rooms. Nancy left and made her way toward Jamison Hall, to invite Bess and George to the party.

The evening was fragrant with the scent of the last blooms. Autumn was right around the corner—Nancy could feel it in the orange light of the harvest moon hovering behind the trees. Soon the leaves would start to turn, and by next month they'd be on fire, peppering the ground like multicolored confetti.

As she reached Jamison Hall's Gothic, arched entrance, Nancy couldn't pull herself out of the funk she had been put in.

It's too late to stay out of it, she decided as she bounded up the steps toward the second floor. Why bother trying to keep my suitemates from feeling uncomfortable by asking questions? They already are.

"Hi, I'm Nancy," she said, introducing herself as she popped her head through the door of Bess's room.

"So?" the girl inside replied in a drawn-out drawl, like a crusty old librarian. She didn't even bother to look up from her organic chemistry textbook.

Ahh, Nancy thought. The not friendly Leslie King.

"I'm Bess's friend," Nancy continued. "From home. She didn't mention me?"

"She may have—I don't remember," Leslie said.

She doesn't *look* that bad, Nancy thought,

shaking her head. Leslie was even pretty, in a prim sort of way. Too bad she was such an iceberg.

"Getting an early start on your classes, I see," Nancy said, not easily intimidated. She stepped inside the room.

Leslie didn't even pretend to respond.

"Well, I just came by to leave this for Bess," Nancy said, waving a piece of red paper with balloons printed along the edges. "It's an invitation to a room-to-room party at Thayer tonight."

Leslie squinted over the top of her book. *"Another* party?" she said, her expression disdainful. "Does Bess do anything else?"

Before Nancy could answer, Leslie was nodding at Bess's bed: "Just leave it there. I'll see that she gets it."

"You know, you're invited, too," Nancy offered, trying to entice her.

Leslie only replied with a curt, humorless smile as she turned back to her book.

"Wow, she is cold," Nancy muttered under her breath, shivering as she shut the door behind her. Then it dawned on her—Leslie must be the reason Bess was so upset. And who could blame her?

Suddenly Nancy felt a lot better, knowing that Bess's troubles weren't so urgent. Leslie was pretty awful, but then pictures of her own roommate flashed across Nancy's mind—Kara tossing clothes left and right over her shoulder, her own purse in Kara's hand. Who didn't have problems at first? Nancy reflected, slipping the party invitation under George's door. "Poor Bess," she murmured. "She'll figure hers out. The only question is, will I figure out mine?"

Pouring herself a cup of punch at the drinks table at the Sigma open house, Bess turned to watch the dancing. It was only her second night at college, but it was already her second frat party. It was kind of strange, she thought, how this one looked exactly like Zeta's.

Strange—or scary? She had to pinch herself. It was creepy how this party already felt like a rerun of the night before, with the same music coming at her from four or five directions, and the exact same crowd. And as much as she smiled, as much as she tried to get into the music, she still couldn't shake the picture of what had happened with Dave.

So why was she here?

"Why *are* you here?" Bess murmured.

The fact was, she'd been so alone the past two days that she was starting to wonder why everyone had told her college was going to be such a blast. Rooming with Leslie was like living with a block of ice. Bess was surprised there wasn't a little wet puddle around her desk. Then again, that would mean Leslie could actually melt. So far, Bess hadn't felt the temperature in their room rise even one degree.

With nothing better to do than stand and

watch, Bess slowly swayed her hips to the pounding beat of the music.

"That's what I like," a voice said behind her. "A girl who enjoys the better things in life."

Bess turned to find one of the Zeta guys she and Dave had passed on the stairway the other night. An arrogant leer was plastered on his face as he looked down at Bess.

She rolled her eyes. "What you like is a girl who breathes."

"What I *really* like is a girl who plays hardball. Dave said you were a hot little cookie."

Automatically, Bess froze. Dave doesn't know a thing about me, she screamed inside her brain.

"Come on, baby, face it, you need me," the guy said, reaching for her.

Instantly Bess came to life, whirling away and running into the crowd.

I need you like I need a hole in the head, Bess thought. Though last night I acted like I had more than a few holes up there.

"Don't let that jerk bother you," another voice said beside her.

Bess peered over her shoulder: another guy— tall and lanky. And kind of sweet looking.

But Dave was sweet looking, too, Bess remembered. At first.

"Do I know you?" Bess asked acidly.

"I—I don't know," the guy replied, suddenly puzzled.

"Are you *another* of Dave's friends?" Bess shot back.

"Dave who?" the guy said, glancing behind him. "Look, I think you're mistaking me for someone else. My name's—"

Bess cut him off with a hostile glare.

"I just thought that maybe you'd like to—"

"Like to *what!*" Bess broke in.

He raised a hand in self-defense. "Wait a second, I didn't mean—"

"Well, what *did* you mean?"

The guy cocked his head, as though at someone speaking a foreign language. Then, defeated, he just laughed and shook his head. "Have a nice life," he said, and walked away. "I guess."

Bess stalked off in a huff, and for the fourth or fifth time that night did a lap around the bottom floor of the jammed fraternity house, praying she'd run into Nancy or George. She lingered around the buffet table, then headed for the dance floor. But she finished her circuit without finding either of her friends.

Where are they? Bess wondered. She was sure they'd be here. Everyone she'd bumped into had said that this party was the one to go to. Every time she'd tried to track them down to tell them about it, they were gone or had something else to do.

Probably off doing something better than this, Bess thought. First, they deserted her and made her move in by herself. Then they ditched her at the Zeta party the first chance they got. It's like they're forgetting all our years of friendship, Bess lamented.

Scowling at every guy who even accidentally looked her way, Bess headed toward the buffet table again. If I'm going to be alone, she rationalized, there may as well be more of me to keep myself company.

But halfway across the cavernous room, she found herself staring straight at Dave. He was dancing with a girl Bess recognized from her dorm. Her fists clenched. Her jaw locked. Her brain was a jumble of thoughts and fears.

I have to warn that girl, Bess thought impulsively. Her mouth opened and then snapped closed silently. Bess wanted to say something, but suddenly she was confused about what had actually happened the night before. Of course Dave had taken advantage of her. He'd known it was her first frat party. He'd made her miserable. But still, Bess couldn't honestly deny that she'd been attracted to him.

Maybe I did lead him on, she found herself thinking. I'm just a clueless little freshman. No! Dave was wrong.

Meanwhile, the girl dancing with Dave turned to Bess, wondering what she wanted. Then she and Bess both stared at Dave. Maybe now he'll apologize, Bess thought.

All he did was look straight through her, as if he'd never laid eyes on her. Then he turned away, shrugged, and pointed back at Bess over his shoulder.

"You know that girl?" he yelled to his date above the music.

The girl just shook her head. Dave chuckled and shrugged and led her away into the crowd.

But you kissed me! Shocked, Bess called out to him in her mind. You liked me!

Dave didn't even look back, and Bess turned and made her way out the door and back to her dorm.

CHAPTER 7

There you are," Nancy heard someone say as she walked out of the stairwell onto the second floor of Thayer.

"Julie?" Nancy said in disbelief. Her suitemate was dressed to kill in a slinky silk sundress, revealing most of what Nancy saw was a very lean—almost too skinny—body. Her eyes were sparkling, her hair wild and frizzy. Nancy couldn't help but be bewildered by her suitemate's transformation from the tired, zoned-out girl of a couple hours ago into the party animal standing before her. Like Jekyll and Hyde, Nancy thought as Julie took her by the hand and towed her into the thick of the party.

What had been planned as a small social gathering had grown into a bash almost as loud and wild as a frat party. The narrow hallway was jammed with students. Someone had set up a pair of waist-high speakers outside his door and was blasting music by a new band from Seattle.

"Isn't this cool?" Julie shouted above the noise, dancing back and forth, sambalike, as she dragged Nancy through the crowd.

Nancy nodded and smiled as the music seeped into her and the cobwebs from this afternoon began to clear away.

"And this," Julie yelled, twirling Nancy around and pointing her in another direction, "is the floor R.A., my good friend Bill Graham, the mad genius scientist."

"Hi, Bill," Nancy said, a little uncertainly, wondering why Julie was taking her on this tour. "I'm—"

"Nancy," Julie blurted out.

Before she could say anything, Nancy's hand was being pumped up and down by a tall, boyishly handsome guy with a pug nose and animated pale green eyes.

"I'm not quite a mad genius scientist yet," he said. "Just your run-of-the-mill chem major. But you must be the famous Nancy Drew."

"Famous?"

"Ah, my good friend Julie here has told me all about you," Bill teased.

"Oh?" Nancy eyed Julie.

"Yeah." Bill laughed. "Julie thinks you're the coolest girl on your floor."

"Way cooler than my pseudosophisticated roommate," Julie sneered.

"Julie!" Nancy exclaimed, checking for Stephanie in case she was in earshot.

"Oh, come on, Nancy, get with the program.

You think I don't see through her mind games? She's so—I don't know—phony." Julie leaned forward and whispered into Nancy's ear. "In fact, just between you and me, Stephanie isn't really the totally honest type. If you know what I mean."

Julie pulled back and winked. She looked right and left, as if searching for a way to escape. Then she was off, a one-woman rhumba line snaking through the crowd.

"Wow," Bill said, shaking his head. "She's a fun kid, but is she always so out of control?"

"No, not always," Nancy replied distractedly, watching Julie twist away. "In fact, not at all."

"Come on, let me do my job as an R.A.," Bill offered. "I'll introduce you to some of my freshmen."

But as soon as Nancy started to follow, she lost sight of him. As she looked around for someone she knew, Nancy thought about the comment Julie had made. What exactly *did* she mean about Stephanie not being honest?

The hallway was hot and loud. Nancy spotted an open door to the right and stepped in to escape the press of bodies. Some guy was sitting on the edge of a desk next to an open laptop computer, decidedly annoyed.

Something caught her eye as she was ready to back out, and she peeked at the titles lining the rows of a small, beautiful mahogany bookshelf. Nancy was interested to see what it held. Hemingway, Faulkner, Shakespeare, a minilibrary of literary classics. Below these was an entire row of biology and medical textbooks. And between two windows hung a poster of Albert Einstein and another of Jonas Salk, the discoverer of the polio vaccine.

"Wow, I wonder what high school this guy came from," Nancy muttered out loud, impressed by the collection of books.

"You want to see my résumé and SAT scores, too?" she heard from behind her. Nancy turned to find the guy on the desk staring at her in a distinctly unfriendly way.

"Sorry," Nancy said. "I didn't know this was yours."

"You mean you wouldn't have talked about me if you knew I was here," he replied acidly.

"I didn't mean anything by what I said," Nancy answered slowly. "I just couldn't help but notice that you don't exactly have the books of a typical freshman."

"Well, thank goodness I'm not a typical freshman!" he exclaimed. "Besides, what books were you expecting? 'The Complete History of Imported Beer in America'? 'How to Stay Out All Night and Still Ace Your Classes in the Morning'?"

Nancy was speechless. Not only was this guy snide and obnoxious, but he was making judgments about her when he didn't know her at all. She pulled herself together and faced him.

"Maybe what I meant was that I was *impressed* by your collection," she said angrily. "Obviously your bookshelf has nothing to do with your social skills—which are very *unimpressive.*"

"I'm sorry to disappoint you," he countered, "but did you consider that I might not be interested in impressing anyone here?"

"Then you have a great four years ahead of you," Nancy remarked, heading for the door. "Good luck."

"I've only got two more," he called after her. "That's the point."

Just inside the doorway, Nancy turned back.

"I'm not a freshman," he explained through gritted teeth, glancing angrily at the commotion outside his door. "I'm a junior, and I'm not supposed to be *here.*"

He sighed loudly and ran his hands through his dark hair. "Look, I'm sorry I snapped at you," he said. "I'm angry and I probably shouldn't take it out on you."

"No, probably not," Nancy agreed warily.

"My name is Peter," he said finally, "Peter Goodwin."

Nancy smiled despite herself.

"Look," he continued, "don't take this personally. It was—nice to meet you. But I hope I won't see you again. I'm expecting a new dorm assignment to come through."

"Nancy Drew," Nancy replied with a crooked smile. "Though it hardly matters. Happy reading, anyway."

Nancy shouldered her way back into the packed hall and scanned the crowd to see if Bess or George had shown up. She definitely understood what made Peter Goodwin so unfriendly. If he'd already had two years of roommate problems, then to end up in a freshman dorm again would be enough to make anyone mad.

There was also something else she couldn't fault Peter Goodwin for, though with his attitude, she hated to admit she'd noticed. Even though he was pretty much a jerk, Peter Goodwin was also incredibly attractive.

What's that noise? Footsteps. Someone's still awake? Where? The stairs. I'll take the stairs. I'll go down one flight.

Everything's so blurry, the lights are swimming. Whew. Here I am on the second floor, where the party was. Wow, that was close. Someone almost caught me. I've got to chill. This is totally uncool. That would have been it. Bang, whammo, bumped out of school real quick.

Come on, kiddo—worry tomorrow. One day at a time. Isn't that what they're always saying? Well, then, tomorrow will take care of itself. Today I need cash. . . .

Ugh, everything's such a mess. Look at this, popped balloons and empty cups everywhere. Cool—the smashed Cheese Doodles are like orange confetti ground into the carpet.

Thank goodness everyone's finally crashed. These guys talked about being such huge partyers, but look at them, total wimpoids, snoring happily in their little beds.

Hey, what's this? An open door? An empty room. How convenient. What's that silver light? A laptop computer? Someone's working this late at night, and on a weekend? Let's see: Summer bio-research project.

Hmm, maybe I should lighten his load a little. But a computer? It's definitely easy pickings. I don't know. The guy may be a nerd, but he's got work to do, and taking a computer's serious.

But cash, kiddo, remember? You have bills to pay, things to do, people to get off your back. You need more stuff. And, hey, the world's full of computers. He'll live.

There, it's small enough to slip under my shirt. . . .

For what seemed like the hundredth time in the last hour, Nancy eyed the door to her room, listening for any signs of life. All she heard was silence.

When she'd come back from the room-to-room party and opened the door, it was dark, so she walked right in. But when she reached for the light, she heard a lot of coughing and giggling, and throat clearing—rather, *two* throats clearing, Kara's and some guy's.

Kara had pleaded for just a few more minutes of privacy, but a few became ten, then thirty, then an hour.

"Thanks a lot, Kara," Nancy murmured through a deep yawn, lowering herself onto the couch in the lounge. It was as if there was nothing beneath her, as she almost sank straight to the floor. She tried to push herself up, but the couch was like a spineless pile of springy cushions—she sank deeper. "Caught in the grips of the Black Hole," she said, and laughed at herself.

Just then three sharp knocks on the door to the lounge startled her. Not only because it was after one in the morning, but because the knocking was so loud.

Nancy slid off the couch, struggled to her feet, and went to the door.

"Peter?" She recognized the junior with the bad temper and sarcastic wit from the second floor and felt a flutter in her stomach. She couldn't help but notice how tall, dark, and handsome he was.

"Hi. Nancy, right?" Peter said, acting flustered himself. "I need to talk to you." He brushed past her and into the little lounge.

Nancy wondered what he could possibly want to talk about after the exchange they'd had earlier. Maybe he wants to apologize, she hoped. He must have realized how rude he was, but couldn't he have waited until morning?

"Wait. Don't sit down on that," Nancy warned.

But it was too late: the spineless couch collapsed under Peter's weight, and Peter was sucked down helplessly. He struggled to sit up straight.

Nancy chuckled, but when she saw Peter's face redden with embarrassment, she offered him a hand. Peter took it and tugged. Nancy stumbled forward, saving herself from falling on top of him by catching herself against the wall. But her face was close enough to feel his breath fan across her cheek and to see how deep brown his eyes were. She was caught for a second, just long enough to realize she liked being that close.

As they both struggled to their feet, Nancy was aware of Peter's effect on her. He made her feel a flicker of excitement in her stomach and at the tips of her fingers—a feeling she wasn't ready to identify.

Instinctively, she clicked on the projector in her brain and rolled a picture of Ned by: his brown hair, soft dark eyes, and gently curving mouth. She was relieved that he was at least as good-looking as Peter.

Smiling politely, she stepped away to put some distance between them.

"I hope the party wasn't too annoying," she said. "I'm still sorry I barged into your room like that."

"Are you," Peter remarked, folding his arms across his chest. Nancy noticed that the tone of his voice was anything but friendly and that he was acting suspiciously.

"What do you mean?" she asked carefully.

"You didn't happen to notice anything special lying around my room, did you?"

"Is this a trick question?" Nancy laughed uncomfortably.

"That's not funny," Peter said.

Nancy frowned. "Well, I wasn't trying to be funny."

Peter tapped his foot impatiently.

"Let me see." Nancy thought hard. *Shakespeare's Collected Works.* I'd say that was pretty special."

"That's not what I mean," Peter snapped, his voice rising. "I mean something worth a lot of money. Something that maybe you'd like for yourself."

"Something that I'd—" Nancy didn't bother to finish the sentence. "Hey, you're really serious," she said.

"You bet I'm serious," Peter replied.

"What exactly are you suggesting?" Nancy asked.

"Did you notice a laptop computer sitting on my desk?"

Nancy thought a second. "Come to think of it, I did."

"It has mysteriously disappeared," Peter snarled. "Along with three months' worth of research!"

Nancy squinted at Peter in disbelief. "You're here because you think I stole your laptop?"

"Well, you *were* the only one who came into my room all night," Peter said suggestively.

"You mean your winning personality didn't attract droves of visitors?" Nancy replied quicker than she could think. But she had an excuse— she felt as if she'd been slapped, and she couldn't believe Peter was accusing her of stealing.

"My winning personality isn't in question here," he countered.

"So you think I'm the type of person who'd steal?" Nancy said. "Especially something as important and obvious as a computer."

"Well, I—"

"And you think I'm so dumb that I wouldn't have known I'd be the prime suspect?" she went on.

Peter didn't answer, and Nancy could tell he was becoming tongue-tied. She was mad at him, but she also felt sorry for him.

"There were probably two hundred people at that party tonight," she said. "Any one of them could have seen that laptop. Were you in your room all night?"

Peter nodded firmly. "I didn't budge. I was reading."

"What about after the party?"

Peter became thoughtful. "After the party I started cleaning up the mess, but there was too much, so I gave up. But I never left the hallway," he insisted. "There's no way anyone could have slipped into my room, unless . . ."

His voice trailed off, and he dropped his head.

"What is it?" Nancy asked.

"I wanted to take advantage of the quiet and do some more reading. But I was thirsty, so I went downstairs to the soda machines in the basement to get a couple cans of—" Peter's gaze locked with Nancy's. "My door—I left it open."

The thief had struck again, Nancy realized. But

this time it wasn't a locket or a bracelet or book money—this time it was an expensive computer.

Peter hung his head. "I'm such an idiot." He lifted his eyes to Nancy's. "In more ways than one."

"Don't worry about it," Nancy replied, though his accusation still stung.

"If I'd only thought about it . . ."

Nancy shrugged. "You were upset."

"I just can't believe it's all gone." He sighed out loud and rubbed his eyes. "Three months' worth of research."

"Didn't you have your stuff backed up on floppy disks?" Nancy asked, surprised.

Peter looked at her wryly. "I didn't have extra disks, and I never got around to buying more. So now you know"—he sighed—"not only am I sometimes a rude jerk, but I'm also a very lazy rude jerk."

For the first time that night Nancy thought she saw a trace of a smile on Peter's face. Then their eyes locked, and another one of those alarm bells went off deep in Nancy's brain. She looked away, confused by how attractive he still seemed even after accusing her of stealing his computer.

"So now what?" Peter muttered.

"The first thing I'd do is tell your R.A. Then report it to campus security."

"You have all the answers, don't you?" Peter said, studying her strangely.

Actually, I don't have any, Nancy thought to herself. But it's time I started to get some. These thefts are spreading, and they're getting more and more serious.

"So . . ." Peter began, searching for conversation. "How's *your* room?"

"I wouldn't know," Nancy replied, rolling her eyes at her door.

"You mean you lost your key already?"

"No." Nancy started to explain, "It's just that—" She looked up, realized what she was about to say, and started laughing. "I probably shouldn't be telling you this—"

"Oh, I get it," Peter said knowingly. "Your roommate's got *company.*"

"Bull's-eye." Nancy smiled. "I don't mind or anything," she quickly added. "But . . ."

"It's one o'clock in the morning, and you're tired, right?"

Nancy nodded. "She said she'd be only a few more minutes, but it's been over an hour."

"Maybe you should knock again. They probably fell asleep."

"I don't want to be rude or anything."

"Suit yourself. But I'm not sure you're the one I'd be calling rude. Don't forget, it's your room, too."

The main door to the suite opened then, and Nancy saw Dawn Steiger standing in the doorway. As R.A., Dawn lived in the suite's only single room. Nancy had seen her in passing when she was helping everyone move in the day before. She was tall and thin, with long, straight, blond hair, a perfect creamy complexion, and sharp, alert eyes. Even in blue jeans and a baggy gray sweatshirt, Nancy thought she looked like a cover girl.

"Hi, Dawn," Nancy began. "This is—"

Before she could say another word, Dawn planted a warm kiss on Peter's lips, then stepped back, her face beaming with joy.

"I see you guys have already met," Nancy said.

"I'm glad you came up to meet the freshmen on your own," Dawn said to Peter. She turned to Nancy. "You guys might be seeing quite a bit of Peter this year."

Even though Peter was holding Dawn tight around her waist, he appeared uncomfortable and embarrassed.

"You should get some sleep," Dawn suggested, taking Peter's hand and leading him toward her room.

"Yeah, I should," Nancy said, eyeing the couch warily. "These have been two of the most fun days of my life, but they've also been the longest."

"And don't forget you have course registration tomorrow," Dawn reminded her. "Take it from me, you'll need all your energy."

Throwing one last, longing glance toward her own door, Nancy lowered herself onto the Black Hole sofa. Just as she was drifting off, she heard a soft laugh coming through Dawn's door. Ned popped into her brain, and she pictured herself and him standing at opposite ends of the hallway. Both of them were smiling. He was walking toward her, and as he came nearer, she could see him mouthing, "I love you." But when he reached out to take her hand, she turned, opened the suite door, and walked through, closing it behind her. Ned knocked and called out to her, but she held her hands over her ears, blocking him out. . . .

Nancy opened her eyes and sat up abruptly. She was breathing fast. She heard another noise from Dawn's room, deep laughter—Peter's.

She was too sleepy to resist the strong swell of emotion that washed over her, chilling her like a wave of icy water. She was thinking about Dawn and Peter. She didn't like what she was feeling, but she knew what it was—jealousy.

CHAPTER 8

George was sitting in the office of the manager of the University Credit Union, gazing out the window. It was a perfect morning, clear and sunny. It was Monday, the first weekday of her new life as a college student, and she had come to pick up the money she needed for books and supplies.

As the manager tapped on his computer keyboard and studied the screen, George swallowed hard. The man wore the expression of someone about to deliver very bad news.

"Isn't the check here?" George asked. "The State Department of Higher Education said—"

"I'm afraid there's a problem with your student loan," the manager said, cutting her off. "Miss—uh—" He glanced worriedly at his computer screen.

"Fayne. George Fayne," George offered.

"Miss Fayne. Yes. You see—well, it's very

strange, really—but it seems that your loan has been frozen."

George cocked her head to one side. "Frozen? What do you mean?"

"It means that for some reason they're enjoining us not to disburse your allotted assets."

George rose a little out of her seat. "They're *what* to not *what* my *what?*"

The manager smiled tightly and cleared his throat. "They're telling us not to give you your money."

"But why?" George leaned across the manager's desk and tried to peer into his computer screen, but the man turned the monitor so she couldn't see.

"Can't I see that?" George asked.

"I'm afraid not."

"But it's me on that computer."

The manager nodded gravely. "I'm afraid it is."

"Can't I see what they're saying about me?"

The manager shook his head.

"But I need that money," George complained.

"I'm afraid, Miss—uh, Miss—"

"Fayne. George Fayne. Are you sure you have my name right? Maybe that's the problem, maybe—"

"We don't use names here," the manager explained with a wave of his hand. "We only use eight-digit numbers."

"Great, I'm just a number."

The manager nodded sadly. "We have to carry

out the computer's orders. You should contact the Department of Higher Education directly and straighten things out with them before we can disburse—I mean, give you your money."

George left the credit union scratching her head, wanting to cry, but laughing to herself instead.

First, I'm not even me anymore, I'm just an eight-digit number, she thought. Then the government tells me I'm about to be arrested because they think I'm a guy. And now they want to take away my money. Wow, whoever's pulling the strings around here must be having a good laugh, pointing to a picture of me and saying, Let's make her life *really* complicated.

"And they're succeeding," she muttered.

"I swear, I swear, I *swear* it won't happen again!" Kara pleaded with Nancy in the doorway of their room. "I meant to kick him out, but we both fell asleep."

"Uh-huh," Nancy replied, failing to keep a straight face. "You just fell asleep."

Kara nodded. "Can you believe it? I guess we had too much partying."

Nancy arched her back and rotated her head, stretching her neck.

Kara winced. "The couch was that bad, huh?"

" 'Bad' would be an understatement," Nancy said.

Kara was horrified. She grabbed Nancy's wrist and stared into her eyes. "You don't really think

I'd lock you out of your own room on the second night of college, do you? Really, we did fall asleep. I mean, we don't even have a system yet."

Nancy stared back at her. "A system?"

"You know—a sock hanging off the doorknob, or an *X* in the upper right-hand corner of our bulletin board." Kara nodded meaningfully. "A signal. So that, you know, we'd know when—when the other person is—"

"Otherwise engaged?" Nancy finished the thought.

"I'm so glad you understand, Nancy. You're the coolest roommate ever. Look, I can't talk it over now. I have to run. I have a date for breakfast."

As Kara ran off through the lounge, she eyed the couch and shook her head. Poor Nancy, she thought. Stuck with me for a whole year. But I guarantee by June, she'll not only love me, she'll *need* me. She just doesn't know it yet.

"What a nut case." Nancy laughed to herself as she watched Kara zigzag to the door. But she had to admit, as annoying as her new roommate was, she could also be likable in her goofy, grin-and-bear-it sort of way.

About to head out herself, Nancy's eyes fell on an open bag of nacho chips on Kara's desk. Her stomach rumbled.

Go ahead, she told herself. You'll need your energy for course registration. Besides, Kara owes you. With a fistful of chips, Nancy headed out of her room, armed with the university course catalog.

From what she remembered of Ned's experience at Emerson, registration was nothing but long lines of confused students. In other words—total chaos. Luckily, her name fell between A and H; she should be able to get it over with early, before the lines got insane.

"Hi, Julie," she said cheerily as she stepped into the hallway.

Julie leaned against the lounge wall in a sweatshirt that fell to her knees. Unlike the night before, when she had been full of energy, she now looked exhausted—like a deflated balloon. Julie managed a kind of half smile and glanced uneasily toward the telephone, where Stephanie was whispering intimately into the receiver.

"Hey," Nancy said, trying to prod Julie to life. Stephanie tossed a sharp, annoyed look at Nancy, who lowered her voice to a whisper. "Aren't you supposed to be getting ready for course registration?"

"Yeah?" Julie stared blankly at Nancy.

"Everyone from A to H is supposed to be at Sage Field House between nine and ten."

Julie thought for a second. "Right, I forgot."

"Come on." Nancy nudged her. "Get your things. I'll wait here."

Nancy watched Julie plod down the hall toward her room. Boy, her brain is working in low gear this morning, she thought.

Julie reappeared dragging her book bag behind her. *I wonder if she's all right?* Nancy thought.

"Are you feeling okay?" she asked gently.

Julie stared at her a moment, obviously confused. "Uh-huh. Why?"

"Well, you seem so tired or—I don't know, run-down," Nancy replied gingerly.

For a minute Julie appeared to want to say something, then stopped as if she'd changed her mind. Finally she answered, "I do get tired easily. I'll have to try to get more sleep," she said uncomfortably. "And remember to take my vitamins."

"Good idea," Nancy agreed. "I suppose we could all use vitamins. We haven't gotten much sleep with all the partying we've been doing."

Nancy hoped sleep and extra vitamins were all that Julie needed and that nothing was seriously wrong with her.

As they were leaving, Nancy could feel Stephanie watching her. She was still on the phone, her hand cupped over the mouthpiece. Thinking she should at least try to be pleasant, Nancy turned back to smile, but Stephanie swung around so Nancy couldn't see her.

Outside, Nancy turned to Julie. "Maybe I'm imagining something," she said as they joined the steady stream of students heading for the field house. "But is there something strange about Stephanie?"

"What do you mean?" Julie asked.

"I'm not sure," Nancy said cautiously. "I can't

put my finger on it. What was it you were saying about her last night—something about her not being honest?"

Julie stopped and cocked her head. "Did I say that?"

"Don't you remember?"

Julie hesitated, acting as if she was trying to decide what to say.

Nancy apologized. "I probably shouldn't have said anything. After all, she is your roommate."

"No, that's okay," Julie said, almost brightly. "But I know what you mean. There *is* something I just don't trust about her. The things she says and the way she takes my stuff without asking for it."

"She borrows your things?" Nancy asked, more interested.

"I wouldn't say *borrow*, exactly," Julie explained.

"You mean without asking?" Nancy prompted.

"And then she doesn't put them back. Things just disappear from my closet and show up in hers. Like she's always had them. And some of my jewelry—"

"Jewelry?"

"Yeah, this necklace I had," Julie said cautiously. "It's like Stephanie doesn't take no for an answer, and she'd do anything to get what she wants."

Would do anything—Nancy turned the thought over in her mind. Stephanie *did* seem pushy. Come to think of it, Nancy realized, every time I see her, she acts more and more as if she's got something to hide. Just like now, the way she was acting so secretive about her phone call.

Julie's eyes were alive now, shifting back and forth as if she were figuring something out.

Maybe she's putting it together, too, Nancy thought. But why would Stephanie take anything? she wondered. She wears such expensive clothes—she doesn't need to steal anything. She can just buy what she wants.

Nancy decided to try one more thing. "Uh, Julie? I need to write some letters, and I was just wondering if you or Stephanie happen to have a computer I could use."

Nancy caught a slight hesitation in Julie's step, almost as though she'd stumbled over a crack in the sidewalk.

"Funny you should ask," Julie began guardedly. "I didn't see Stephanie unpack a computer when she moved in, but she mentioned something about one last night, after the party. It was late, so I don't really remember what she said. But it was something about a computer—I'm sure of that. Something about a laptop."

Nancy's mind started racing, trying to match her first impressions of Stephanie with her suspicions. They all funneled into one clear thought: she wasn't surprised.

Something was still bugging her, though. It was too easy. It just didn't make sense.

"I can't wait until our own phones are working," George said angrily as she dropped another quarter into the pay phone in the basement of her dorm. "It took a half hour for this one to become free."

"Thank you for calling the Illinois State Department of Higher Education," the operator's voice said evenly.

George cleared her throat. "Yes, I'd like to speak with—"

"If you know your party's extension—"

"No, I need to—" George replied politely.

"Press one now."

"Uh, hello?"

"Press two now."

George scowled at the pay phone and pressed 2.

"Thank you," the same operator said.

"Yes, I need to speak with—"

"If you'd like to speak with—"

"Student loans," George cried.

"Press three now."

George pressed 3.

". . . Four now."

"Okay, okay!"

George pressed 4. Or was that 5? She forgot! Or maybe her finger slipped, or it missed entirely. She was stuck in "Phone Space" and was drifting farther and farther away from human contact.

The way things were going lately, it was almost not surprising that she couldn't make sense of this message. Right now, she had no idea where her call was going. For all she knew, it was headed for New Jersey.

The only way to be sure was to hang up and start all over again. But that was like returning to the back of a traffic jam.

"Thank you," the operator returned after a few minutes, speaking in that syrupy synthetic twang. "All representatives are currently busy. Please stay on the line and your call will be answered by the next available operator."

"Ugh," George moaned, and let her forehead fall forward and bump against the cold metal of the phone box. Computer-generated elevator music began to seep into her ear. Synthesized violins and cellos and trumpets. George imagined musicians in tuxedos using computers for instruments, tapping out the notes on their little keyboards.

"I need to talk to a human being," George snapped.

The phone line bristled to life: "Thank you for your patience—"

"Oh, thank goodness," George said. "Can I please speak to someone about my—"

"Your call is important to us," the operator continued. "Please stay on the line." The music started again where it had left off.

George's hands were shaking with frustration. She glanced nervously at her watch. It was a quarter to ten. She was going to miss registration. Everyone from A to H had to register within the next fifteen minutes.

"Great," George cried. "Not only am I about to be arrested, not only am I flat broke, but now I'm not even going to get the classes I want."

The elevator music was cut short. Another tranquilizing voice slipped into her ear: "Thank you for your patience—"

George held the phone away and blurted out, "You're not welcome," and slammed it into the cradle. But just before it hit, she heard a tiny voice call out.

"Hello? Anybody there? May I help you?"

It sounded almost human!

George grabbed at the phone again but it was too late—nothing but a dial tone.

"I'm not mad," George said, struggling to persuade herself. "I'm a fugitive, I'm broke, and now I'm not registered for any classes. But I'm not mad—"

As George pushed on the phone booth doors, she noticed her hands were balled into fists. How do you argue with someone you can't even see or talk to? she wondered helplessly.

As she shoved her way through the doors, all she could think about was sprinting to the gym to go a couple of rounds with a punching bag. Then, *wham*. She had run into the chest of a very muscular guy wearing a T-shirt and shorts.

Rubbing her squashed nose, she looked up and was even more stunned by what she saw than by the ache in the middle of her face. There was a gleaming white smile, a pair of intelligent almond-shaped eyes, high cheekbones, and silky black hair. She was toe to toe with the guy from the quad, and close up he was more than simply good-looking—he was breathtakingly gorgeous!

The registrar shook her head at her computer monitor. "I'm sorry, but Eighteenth-Century Women Writers is already full."

"Already?" Nancy exclaimed, disheartened. "But registration isn't even an hour old."

The registrar smiled. "Unfortunately, upper-classmen get to register during the summer by mail. And Caldwell is one of the most popular professors we have. I don't think we've gotten a freshman into that class in five or six years."

Nancy bit down on her pencil. It's okay, she told herself. She quickly ran a finger down her list of classes that looked the most interesting.

"Okay," she tried. "How about The Modern American Novel, Professor Herrin, Mondays and Wednesdays at ten?"

The registrar shook her head sadly, not even bothering to look it up. "Look at it this way—at least you know you have good taste."

"Too bad good taste won't get me into the electives I want," Nancy murmured. "Well, at least I can get into the intro classes I need, right?" she asked. "Those are pretty much de-signed for freshmen, aren't they?"

"Well," the registrar said, "not necessarily. There are a few intro classes that are very pop-ular with upperclassmen, such as Hospitality 120. That's a class on wines. We have a two-year waiting list for that one. And, of course, you need to be twenty-one. Then there's Journalism 100, Investigative Reporting, with Professor McCall—"

"Wait a minute," Nancy cried, a sinking feeling in her stomach. "Journalism 100 is full? But that's going to be my major. I *have* to take that class!"

"Well, it was full yesterday," the registrar said. "But I'll look again just to make sure." She tapped a few keys on her computer. "Wait a minute," she said, "there's one spot left. There must have been a cancellation."

"Did she say there's a place in Journalism 100?" the guy in line next to Nancy asked suddenly.

"No, she didn't," Nancy cried quickly, leaning in to the registrar. "Push that button," she whispered in a panic. "That spot is mine!"

Five minutes later she was shielding the sun from her eyes, looking for Julie in the crowd of milling students. There were a few things about Stephanie she had to know. She was determined to start putting the puzzle together, or at least to gather a few of the bigger pieces.

There was no sign of Julie, but she did spot Eileen and Reva hanging out under a tree next to the parking lot.

"Hi, guys," she said, taking a seat in the grass beside them.

"Hey, did you see this, Nancy?" Reva asked,

sliding over a special orientation edition of the college newspaper, *The Wilder Times.*

Stretched across the top in bold type was the headline "Freshman Overdose Victim Out of Danger."

Nancy read the opening paragraph.

Freshman Joanne Matlock, who was carried unconscious from the Zeta party Friday night, is resting comfortably in the infirmary at the university's Garrett Health Center. She still refuses to reveal who her drug supplier is. An anonymous source confirms that it is a Wilder University student.

"I heard about this girl," Nancy said, tapping her finger on the photo of the girl in the paper. "Wow, she's really pretty."

"Yeah, well, it didn't do her much good," Eileen said, shaking her head. She leaned forward, lowering her voice. "Over breakfast I heard some gossip about the guy this Joanne is supposedly dating. He's a junior who seems to be Control Central when it comes to scoring drugs on campus."

"Anyway," Reva said, glancing at her watch and pushing herself to her feet. "It's registration time, Eileen."

Eileen anxiously asked Nancy, "What's it like?"

"A total zoo," Nancy answered, and gave her a quick pat on the back.

Reva nodded soberly. "Exactly. Ready for battle, soldier?"

Eileen nodded. "Aye aye, sir," she said, and saluted.

"Good luck, you guys," Nancy called, turning in the other direction.

When Nancy reached Thayer Hall, she checked her watch. It was about ten-thirty.

"Keats." She mumbled Stephanie's last name, trying to remember the registration schedule. A through H from nine to ten, she recalled. I through R from ten to eleven.

Nancy began to run. She needed to check out Stephanie and Julie's room, and she had only thirty minutes to get in, poke around, and get out.

Only the third day of college and you're already risking everything, Nancy thought to herself as she took the stairs two at a time. If anyone catches you breaking in, everyone's going to think *you're* the thief.

Nancy slowed to a walk when she reached her floor, her heart pounding.

You have to do it, Nancy prodded herself. Stephanie will never cooperate or admit to anything. You've got to find out for yourself. One way or another.

A woman wearing a green smock was vacuuming the hallway outside the suite as Nancy approached. The suite door was wide open. Nancy smiled and said hello, but just as she stepped in, she stopped short and whirled back around.

Something had glinted in the light—something familiar. Nancy gawked at the woman's throat and pointed.

It was the last thing in the world she expected to see.

"That's my locket!" Nancy cried.

CHAPTER 9

"Please believe me," the woman pleaded. With quivering hands she unhooked the locket from around her neck. "I didn't steal it. I found it outside in the trash."

"In the trash?" Nancy quizzed her.

"The Dumpster—outside—there." She pointed at the wall, as if it were invisible and you could see the big green Dumpster by the back door down below.

The woman looked upset. "Please don't tell anybody."

Nancy laid a gentle hand on her shoulder. "Just tell me when you found it," she said soothingly.

"It was yesterday. No, the day before yesterday. I was emptying the trash—"

"The trash from *this* suite?" Nancy said in disbelief.

"Y-yes," the woman stammered. "I saw it flashing in the sun, like this—" She held up the gold charm and let the shiny metal glint in the light. "I didn't know why someone would want to throw out such a beautiful thing."

She saw Nancy frowning and seemed ready to cry. "Please, if you say something, I'll lose my job. Please—take it, I don't want it!" she implored, dumping the locket and chain into Nancy's hand.

Nancy believed the woman. After all, if she had stolen it, she definitely wouldn't have worn it. But the maid's discovery of the locket in the trash from the suite added more proof to Nancy's belief that the thief had to be one of her new suitemates.

"It's okay." She nodded. "It's just between us."

"Thank you, thank you," the woman said, and wiped her eyes.

Puzzled, Nancy stepped quietly inside the suite, clutching the chain of Ned's locket in one hand. She listened for anyone, but there wasn't a sound. Everyone's probably at registration, she decided.

She turned the heart over and over, letting the light play across the gold. She thought she'd be happy to see it again, but what she felt instead was confusion. Now that she had it back, she had a choice to make—wear it or not?

She pried it open and stared at the tiny picture of Ned that he'd put inside. It was a face she knew almost as well as her own. For the first time, Nancy understood clearly that the locket was more than a piece of jewelry with a photo inside. It was a symbol. If she wore it, they belonged to each other. If she didn't, they didn't. It was that simple.

I can't make this decision now, Nancy thought to herself, shaking her mind free of Ned. I have work to do.

She shoved the locket into her pocket and turned slowly toward the bedrooms. When she reached Stephanie and Julie's door, her heart was pounding with anticipation. Maybe it wasn't too late to find some of the other missing items.

Standing on her toes, Bess craned her neck, trying to spot Nancy or George in any of the registration lines snaking through the field house. But it was hopeless. The place was packed.

Nancy and George have probably been done for an hour now, Bess decided. Again, they didn't bother to wait for me. They're too wrapped up in their own stuff to care what courses I take. Or anything else about me, for that matter, Bess thought, remembering the invitation Leslie had handed her that morning.

Leslie had said Nancy had dropped the invitation off late the night before, well after Bess had gone out. It was so last-minute, it was painfully obvious to Bess that Nancy brought it over because she thought she had to, not because Nancy really wanted her to come.

Nearly at the head of the line, Bess took a deep breath and warily eyed the course catalog in her hands. It was as thick as a big-city telephone book—and almost as interesting, she thought. Okay—decision time, she commanded herself, flipping to the front and running her finger down the list of freshman requirements. This semester, she thought, I have to take calculus and Western Civ I.

Bess fanned the catalog to the back page. She'd managed to jot down a few more course possibilities before disturbing thoughts about Dave distracted her.

"Name, please," the registrar was saying.

Bess looked up, flustered. "Uh—Bess Marvin?"

The registrar smiled crookedly. "Are you asking me or telling me?"

"Telling—I guess."

"Then you're in the wrong line. M and N is the next one over. This is K and L."

The next line was so long it trailed out the field-house doors. "Can't I just register here anyway?" Bess pleaded.

The registrar shrugged. "Those are the rules," she said. "And there are signs everywhere. Most people see them. Step aside, please. Next!"

As Bess slinked away, she wanted to crawl under a rock. She was sure everyone was staring at her, so she was forced to smile as though she knew exactly what she was doing. Inside, she felt as clueless and stupid as Dave had said she was.

Maybe what I really need is to start all over, she pondered, just go back to River Heights and pretend the last three days never happened.

Then she realized what a stupid idea that would be, and how impossible it would be to explain to her parents, and to Nancy and George.

An hour later, after finally registering, she was back outside, leaning against a tree and squinting up at the sky, trying not to cry.

"Not so easy, is it?" a voice said from behind her.

Bess wanted to turn and run, but something about that voice anchored her feet to the ground. Something gentle and courteous. She shrugged. "I guess," she said weakly.

She heard a gentle laugh. "I was behind you, also in the wrong line. In fact, I was over an hour late. It's the story of my life. I only got one course I wanted."

"I didn't even get one," Bess whispered, her eyes drying at the thought that she wasn't the only bumbler at Wilder. She slowly turned around, and even with everything on her mind, Bess was surprised at the warm rush of feeling that invaded her. Standing in front of her was a lean, boyishly handsome guy, with straight blond hair and green eyes that were dazzling in the sunlight. He had a killer smile—straight white teeth, dimples and all.

"Brian Daglian," he said, holding out his hand.

"Um—Bess Marvin," Bess offered shyly. His cheerfulness was so contagious, Bess found herself grinning despite herself.

"Now, that's more like it," Brian said. "You're beautiful when you smile, do you know that?"

"I am?" Bess replied in disbelief. The compliment actually seemed genuine, not like some pickup line.

"Trust me," Brian said, and winked. "It's funny, isn't it," he continued, "my parents keep telling me that these are going to be the best four years of my life. I don't know about you, but the last three days have been anything but for me."

Bess nodded.

"So, how'd you make out?" Brian asked.

Bess sighed. "A biology class with some guy named Ross was the best I could do. I really wanted Drama One with Professor Hodge, but I didn't have a chance."

"No way," Brian said excitedly. "That's the one class I *did* get. There must have been a cancellation. Our moons were probably in the same house."

Bess was puzzled.

"That's astrology talk for karma." Brian laughed.

"Karma," Bess repeated skeptically, and shrugged. "Anyway, you got one thing you wanted, remember?"

"Yeah, one thing, but I had to fall back on my old standby—Advanced Latin for another of my courses." Brian took a classical actor's stance and recited a few lines of what could have been poetry in Latin.

Brian was funny. And it didn't escape Bess that his performance was pretty good. "Do you really act?" she asked.

• "A little," he said, his eyes sliding shyly away. "But, hey—what do you say we go drown our sorrows in a couple of double-thick milk shakes at the snack bar?"

"What? You mean you want to go with *me?*" Bess asked, taken aback.

Brian quickly whirled around, then around again, like a dog chasing his tail. "I don't see anyone else standing here," he said, erupting into cheerful laughter.

Bess couldn't believe her luck. Brian was really sweet and totally hot—just her style.

Hold on there, you've only known him for five minutes. Bess caught herself, remembering that Dave had also seemed really nice at first. Still, Brian was definitely the best thing about Wilder so far.

"There's nothing right now that would make me happier," she said enthusiastically, and fell into step beside him.

Looking left and right down the empty passageway, Nancy delicately jiggled the lock to Julie and Stephanie's door with a metal nail file. In under ten seconds the knob had turned smoothly in her palm and she was slipping inside her suitemates' room. That was easy, she thought. It wouldn't take a genius to break into these rooms.

The window blinds were closed, so the room was dark. Not daring to turn on a light, she squinted through the shadows. She couldn't remember which side was Julie's and which was Stephanie's. Then she spied a pair of studded black cowboy boots backed against the right wall. They were a dead giveaway—definitely Stephanie's style. Nancy made a beeline for the right-hand closet.

Inside, she found ten black T-shirts, four black minis, two pairs of black high-tops. It's a good thing Stephanie and Liz don't live together, Nancy thought. They'd never be able to tell their clothes apart.

At the back, Nancy noticed a slew of expensive-looking, skimpy dresses—but nothing incriminating.

"Well, I've come this far," Nancy murmured, eyeing the top drawer of Stephanie's dresser. "I may as well go all the way."

The drawers were a perfect place to hide valuables, big enough, even, for a laptop computer. Nancy slid them open one by one and swept the bottoms with her hand. She didn't feel anything besides socks and underwear and piles of silky nightgowns.

As her eyes rested on the bottom drawer, Nancy shook her head. I can't believe I didn't notice this before, she thought.

The drawer was secured with a heavy-duty padlock.

I guess everyone has a right to a safe place for their things, Nancy reflected. As rude and secretive as Stephanie had been, even she deserved the benefit of the doubt—if only just this once.

I can settle this one way or another, Nancy

thought, knowing she hadn't met a padlock she couldn't pick.

Until now, she decided as she lifted the lock. It was the kind that needed a specially shaped key. Her picking abilities would be useless.

"Now, why would Stephanie need a high-security lock on her dresser drawer?" Nancy wondered. She glanced over her shoulder at the pricey wardrobe hanging in Stephanie's closet. What's she hiding? And why would she need to steal? It just doesn't add up. Is it some sort of compulsion?

Suddenly Nancy heard footsteps outside the door—a key scraping against a lock. She froze.

Please let it be someone else's room, she prayed.

As she whipped around, she saw that her prayer had gone unanswered—the doorknob was turning!

CHAPTER 10

Nancy wanted to sink through the floor as the door opened. Caught breaking into someone else's room, she thought to herself. Now everyone will think *I'm* the thief!

Someone stepped into the room. Nancy was ready to face whoever had come in, and when she saw who it was, she breathed a sigh of relief. It was Julie. But in the dark, Julie didn't recognize her. Her face went absolutely white, her eyes wild, scanning the room. "Who are you? Help!"

"Julie!" Nancy cried. "It's me, it's Nancy."

"Nancy?" Julie asked, stepping forward into the shadows. "B-but—what are you doing in here?"

"Julie, it's not what you think—"

She bolted toward her closet and dresser. When she found them untouched, she whirled around. "Why are you here?" she cried. "This is *my* room!"

"Do you remember what you were telling me about Stephanie?" Nancy said.

"You've been going through my things?" Julie asked, furious.

Nancy took a step forward. "No, Julie, it's Stephanie's stuff I was going through."

"Stephanie?" Julie blinked. She was nervously tapping her foot, drumming her fingers on her arms.

Why is she so jumpy? Nancy wondered. *I'm* the one who was caught.

"Remember what you were saying about Stephanie this morning," Nancy said, "that she wasn't very trustworthy?"

Julie nodded her head.

"Well," Nancy went on. "I thought that maybe I should just check her out. I'm not saying," she said hurriedly, "that I *know* Stephanie is the thief—"

"But you think she might be?" asked Julie.

"Well—maybe," Nancy admitted. "But I didn't really find any evidence, except that padlock she bolted onto her dresser drawer. Do you know why Stephanie—"

Julie cut her off. "I have no idea," she answered quickly.

"No idea?" Nancy asked in disbelief.

"None." Julie shrugged.

That's weird, Nancy thought. She seemed to have so much to say about Stephanie this morning.

Nancy noticed Julie's lips were trembling.

"Julie, are you okay? You seem—"

"I seem *what?*" Julie shot back accusingly.

"I don't know, sort of in a hurry standing still."

"But, Nancy," Julie said, changing the subject. "I don't understand how you got in here."

Nancy cleared her throat nervously. "It wasn't hard," she replied vaguely.

"Well, you certainly seem skilled at breaking in," Julie said, folding her arms across her chest.

Neither of them said anything for a minute, as though sizing each other up, figuring out what to do next. Julie flipped the light switch, illuminating the room.

Nancy caught her breath. There was a fresh purple bruise blooming under Julie's right eye.

"Julie, what happened to your face?"

"What?" Julie turned quickly away. "What are you talking about?"

"That bruise. Are you okay? Did someone hit you?"

"Hit me!" Julie exclaimed. "I just—I fell on the steps outside—last night—"

"Last night?" Nancy asked dubiously. "But I was with you this morning, and I didn't see any bruise."

"Oh, right," Julie said, catching herself. "Did I say last night? I meant just now, running back to the dorm. I'm such a klutz," she said. "I'm really sorry."

"You didn't do anything wrong," Nancy assured her, stepping over to look more closely at

Julie's face. "Hey, maybe you should get that checked out."

Julie whirled out of Nancy's reach. "I'm fine, I'm fine. I'll see you later, okay?" she insisted, jerking her head toward the door, indicating that Nancy should leave.

Out in the hallway, Nancy breathed a deep sigh. Part of her was even more confused and concerned. I can't figure Julie out, she thought to herself. One minute she's friendly and shy, then the next she's about to jump out of her skin. Could Julie be afraid of Stephanie? Is that what's making her act so odd? Maybe she knows something she's afraid to tell.

Nancy mentally started matching up her suspicions with the bits and pieces of clues she'd found so far. The fact was, she still didn't have a thing on Stephanie except Julie's remarks about her—and the padlock on Stephanie's drawer.

"Well, if Stephanie *is* the thief," she thought aloud as she headed for her room, "then I'm in trouble." Leaning heavily against her door, she shook her head. "She's too smart to get caught."

"And I thought the field house was noisy," Bess said as she scanned Java Joe's for George. Every seat was taken, and almost everybody was shouting to be heard above the boom box blaring music from behind the counter.

"Come on, George," she mumbled, her eyes checking out table after table. "Where are you?"

Finally she spotted her cousin at the door.

"Bess, there you are," George called.

As Bess twisted her way toward her cousin, she thought there was something different about her. It wasn't her clothes, or her hair. It was her expression. George was glowing.

"George, don't smile so hard," Bess said when she reached her. "You're going to hurt yourself."

"I have something incredible to tell you!" George said excitedly.

"I have something to tell you, too," Bess replied, more soberly.

After Brian had left her, Bess decided she was finally ready to talk about what had happened with Dave. Even though she still wasn't sure whose fault it was, maybe talking it out with someone she trusted would help her understand it better. Just the idea of getting it off her chest gave her an enormous sense of relief.

She'd tried calling Nancy's suite, but didn't get an answer. She finally got George, who told Bess she'd meet her in ten minutes. That was almost half an hour ago.

"Come on," George said, grabbing her by the hand. "It's a great day. Let's sit outside."

It certainly was beautiful, Bess had to admit. The bright, clear day was partly the reason Bess had felt ready to talk. After she and Brian had gotten their milk shakes, Brian insisted they drink them while walking laps around the main quad. "It's too nice a day to waste," he'd said, then went on to tell her jokes and sing her songs.

He was like a private, one-man party, quirky and cute and undeniably handsome.

"So—guess what," George said, pulling Bess down beside her in the shade of a huge maple tree.

Bess didn't even have a chance to open her mouth.

"I met somebody," George said breathlessly.

"I met somebody, too," Bess replied, a little more low-key. "I think I did. I mean—I hope I did."

That wasn't what she'd wanted to say. Brian was great, but he wasn't what she'd called George about.

"His name is Will Blackfeather," George said excitedly.

"Blackfeather," Bess repeated. "What a cool name. But look, George, there's—"

"He's really interesting. That's why I was late," George explained. "We talked for hours, and then you called, but he kept telling me more and more about himself—he's Native American, Cherokee—and I lost track of the time."

"That's really great," Bess cut in. "But there's something important I wanted to talk to you about. The other night, at that party—"

"I saw you dancing with that guy," George said. "You looked like you were having a great time."

I did? Bess thought. Then she remembered—that was *before*. But before what? She wasn't even sure anymore. She'd replayed the scene over in her brain so many times. For all she knew, it was *she* who'd tried to push Dave—

"But, George," Bess said, trying to explain, "after that, Dave asked me to take a walk with him, and—"

"Wow, that's really sweet." George smiled at her. "He must really like you."

Bess slowly lay back on the grass. She saw where this was headed. She was finally ready to talk about Dave, but George's head was stuck in the clouds. She'd never seen her cousin so excited about a guy before. The last thing Bess wanted to do was drag her back down to earth.

"Wow," she replied automatically, barely hearing something about Will's family being from South Dakota.

The weight on her chest returned as Bess realized she was still going to have to carry around her sadness.

Let George enjoy herself, Bess decided. At least one of us is happy.

What was George saying now?

"He's a sophomore, George? Really?"

As Nancy passed through Thayer's lobby, she glanced at the dining hall board. Monday Lunch Special: Barbecued Beef on a Bun.

Her stomach moaned. It was one of her favorite meals. But glancing at her watch, she knew she'd just missed lunch.

"I can't believe it's almost four!" she murmured. The afternoon had really flown by. After her run-in with Julie, she'd remembered the two o'clock date she'd made with Paul, the guy she'd met at the Zeta party Friday night. She didn't have the same enthusiasm she'd had when she agreed to their campus tour. Distracted by the thefts, she actually considered canceling the date. But at the last second she went through with it, and to her surprise, she had a really great time.

Paul's short tour had spilled over into an entire afternoon of conversation and discovery. He'd shown her the really quiet, isolated study carrels in the library. He'd told her the scuttlebutt on the university's brand-new fourteen-floor science library. It was sinking at the rate of one inch per year, because the world-famous architect who'd designed it had forgotten to add in the weight of the hundreds of thousands of books. And he'd taken her into the Underground, a dingy, not very special cafeteria by day, which at night was transformed into an atmospheric hangout for the university's more artsy upperclassmen. This was the place where students came to hear and play their original music, recite their poetry, or put on plays.

As Nancy climbed the steps toward her floor, she thought that she definitely liked Paul and that he'd make a great friend. She didn't feel much of a spark for him, though.

Not that I'm looking for one, of course, she reminded herself, thinking of Ned. She felt a huge sense of relief: her wavering feelings about

Ned were hard enough to cope with without someone else complicating matters.

Inside her suite, the lounge was clouded over in a smoky haze. Stephanie was lounging on the couch with some guy, both of them dressed in black leather, as if they'd just come back from a bikers' convention. The ashtray on the coffee table was already choked with their butts.

"Hi, Stephanie," Nancy said, wondering if there was a rule about smoking.

"Here," Stephanie said. She blithely pushed a piece of paper toward her with the toe of her cowboy boot. "Somebody called or something."

"Three times?" Nancy exclaimed, seeing three messages scrawled in three different handwritings. When she picked up the paper, she winced.

Oh, no, she realized. I forgot again.

The first message just said: "Ned, 9 A.M."; the second one: "Ned, 2:30, worried—where are you?"; and the third: "Ned, 3:30 P.M."

"Great," Nancy murmured. "That's all I need."

Then she thought of something and looked at the time on the first message again. Nine A.M., she pondered. Isn't that right when Julie and I were leaving for registration?

She leveled a suspicious gaze at Stephanie, recalling that was just about the time Stephanie was having her very secretive phone conversation.

"Hey, Stephanie," Nancy said, and held up the piece of paper. "Did you take this first message?"

Stephanie squinted at the paper and cocked

her head, as if she'd never seen it before. She turned her attention on the guy.

"Don't look at me," he said with a shrug.

"I guess it was me, then," Stephanie said.

"Weren't you on the phone when I was leaving the suite this morning?" Nancy shot back testily.

Stephanie grinned mischievously. "Well, yes, I believe I was."

Nancy's voice rose a little with irritation: "With Ned?"

Stephanie nodded vaguely. "That was the name he gave."

Nancy crossed her arms guardedly. "Then why didn't you tell me it was him?" she demanded, her blue eyes flashing. "I walked right by you."

"Well, you looked so—I don't know—focused," Stephanie replied coolly. "I didn't want to hold you up."

What is she up to? Nancy wondered. "Unfortunately, I don't have time to argue with you about it now."

As Nancy reached for the phone, Stephanie cleared her throat. "We still can't make outgoing calls," she reminded Nancy with a wide, victorious grin. "Not until next week."

Groaning, Nancy slammed down the receiver and headed downstairs to the pay phones. But halfway out the door, the suite's phone began to ring.

Even though Stephanie was sitting right next to it, she let it ring three or four times before lazily picking it up. "Hello?" she drawled. "Oh, hi. How was your day? Did you get that class you wanted? Really? That's so great. . . . Yeah, she finally came back. Here she is."

Stephanie gazed up at Nancy, the picture of innocence. "It's for you. It's Ned."

Nancy snatched the phone from Stephanie's hand.

"Nancy, this is the second time you promised to call and didn't," Ned said, not trying very hard to mask his frustration.

Nancy glared at Stephanie, who rolled her eyes at her friend. "Come on," she said, slowly getting to her feet. "Nancy needs to have a little chat with her boyfriend."

Nancy took a big breath as she watched Stephanie and her leather-jacketed friend disappear into her room.

"Ned, I'm really sorry," Nancy began as lovingly as she could. "I just got your messages a minute ago. This morning, when you called, Stephanie—"

"Don't blame it on her," Ned said. "Stephanie's a nice girl. At least she talks to me. You're lucky to have her for a roommate."

Nancy shook her head in disbelief. From the cutting tone of Ned's voice, it was obvious that he was ready for a fight. And unless she calmed down, he was going to have one. "Look, Ned, Stephanie's not my roommate—"

"I don't care about Stephanie," Ned interrupted. "Where were you?"

All right, Nancy thought. Have it your way.

"This morning I just didn't have the time," she explained a little testily. "I had to go to registration."

"What about your promise to me?" Ned complained.

Nancy was willing to be patient. She'd promised herself when she left for college that she'd give Ned time to get used to the idea of her having her own life. She even knew that it wouldn't be easy. But what she couldn't have known was how much his hurt and impatience would get under her skin.

"Come on, Ned," she said. "Don't you remember how crazy your life was your first few days at college?"

"That was your excuse last night."

"It's not an excuse, it's a reason," Nancy said firmly. "And there's something else going on, too," she added quickly.

Nancy could hear Ned suck in his breath. "Is it another guy, Nancy?"

Another guy! Nancy thought in disbelief. Does it have to be someone else? Can't it just be me? I'm trying to explain what's going on, but all he wants to hear is that I think about him day and night. But I won't lie. It's just not true. Not anymore.

"Ned, you don't have any idea of what's going on here, so it's not fair for you to accuse me of—"

"Of what, ignoring me? Pretending I don't

143

exist so you can get on with your new college life?"

Nancy was speechless. There was something in Ned's voice she had never heard before. Something that was more than jealousy.

"Look, Ned," she said slowly and forcefully, "I don't know what you're imagining, but it's way off base. I didn't get your messages until a couple of minutes ago, and if you don't believe me, I can't help it. There's also something happening in the suite that's serious, and it's taking a lot of my time. You obviously don't want to hear about it."

Nancy could feel the hot tears flooding her eyes. Sad tears? Angry tears? She didn't know. But she did know how she felt.

Her knees were beginning to feel weak. She leaned back against the wall and brushed her jeans pocket with her hand. She felt the outline of Ned's locket through the cloth and quickly reached up to her neck. It was still bare. She hadn't put the locket back.

Funny, she thought sadly, my heart seems to be making a decision without telling my head.

"I have to start making friends, Ned," she went on. "I'm the one who has to live here."

Taking a big breath, not even knowing what would come next, she continued slowly. "So if all this is a problem for you, then maybe we shouldn't talk for a while. It's not what I want, but maybe it's what we need."

The silence on the other end of the phone was

complete. Nancy was biting her lip. She knew she sounded harsh, but it felt good to be honest. She and Ned were growing up and maybe growing apart, too.

Still, a huge part of her was hoping he'd disagree, hoping he'd see that she was right, and that he needed to be more understanding. But the second Ned started speaking, her hope faded away.

"Maybe you're right," Ned said sadly. "I'll talk to you—sometime, I guess."

"I'll try to give you a call later on."

"Don't make any promises you can't keep," Ned said.

"Okay."

" 'Bye."

" 'Bye."

As Nancy hung up the phone, she felt as if her insides had been hollowed out. It was an alien feeling—this emptiness. The only times she felt this way were when she thought about her mother, who had died when she was three. She didn't want to exaggerate this fight with Ned, but Nancy knew it was serious and that their relationship was in real trouble.

Blinking away her tears, she headed for the privacy of her room.

She took the locket out of her jeans pocket and studied it in the light. She needed to sort out her thoughts, to separate what was going on here at school from her feelings about Ned. But Ned and the thief and her new life at Wilder were all tangled together, like a ball of string.

She slid the locket under some papers in her top desk drawer, where it would be safe but where she wouldn't have to see it for a while. Then she sat in her desk chair and took Ned's picture in her hands. She'd never have believed what her next thought would be, but there it was: Am I going to have to live without you, Ned?

CHAPTER 11

Peter blindly aimed the remote control at the TV in Thayer's game and commons room, channel-surfing his way to distraction.

Depressed about losing an entire summer's worth of biology research, the last thing Peter wanted to think about was Dawn. Unfortunately, he saw her everywhere—in commercials on TV, on the pages of the women's magazines strewn over the game room tables. Not Dawn exactly, but some beautiful, long-legged, blond-haired, blue-eyed model selling soap or shampoo—or worse, skimpy bikinis. They all had her killer body; they all had her sculpted face.

So what's your problem, Goodwin? he taunted himself. She's everything you ever dreamed of: smart, sexy, funny—

Peter moaned and killed the TV. You came here to become a doctor, and now look at you—you've become some Don Juan wannabe who spends his time with a beautiful woman instead of hitting the books. You're just a zombie in front of the boob tube.

And what happened to your oath, he interrogated his own reflection in the TV screen, to never get involved again—especially after last time?

A group of big-time jocks with their usual pack of adoring girls headed for the pool tables in the back.

"Why not?" Peter murmured, pushing himself up from the couch and lifting a cue stick off the wall. "Nothing like a little solo pool to take your mind off things."

But as he racked and broke and watched the balls ricochet across the green felt, all he saw were Dawn's loving eyes roaming all over him. A picture of what had happened last night in her room flashed before him, and he winced. Idiot, he seethed. Those who don't learn from history are doomed to repeat it.

"Hello." A female voice interrupted his reverie.

Peter turned and found himself peering into a familiar face—into the intelligent blue eyes that had glared back at him last night in retaliation for his false accusation.

"Nancy Drew," the girl reminded him. "The notorious thief, remember?"

"How could I forget?" Peter replied, his face reddening with embarrassment. "I can't tell you how sorry I am," he added quickly.

Nancy held up her hand and smiled good-naturedly. "I've forgotten all about it."

Peter cocked his head with wonder. "You're letting me off the hook pretty easily."

"Must be because I've had so much exposure to your charming side," she teased. "Besides, what's the point of rubbing it in? I know I'm not the thief, and you still don't have your laptop."

Peter found himself nodding, trying to catch a glimpse of Nancy without being too obvious. There's definitely something different about her, he mused. Fascinating, but she's already involved, he quickly reminded himself. Dawn had told him Nancy had a serious, longtime boyfriend.

Besides, he chastised himself, what were you just saying about women?

"So . . ." Peter said, grasping for anything to say. "What are you up to?"

"I was just walking around, trying to clear my head," Nancy replied.

"Me, too," Peter murmured. "So I gather there haven't been any developments on our little crime spree?" he probed. "No computers found, for instance?"

"Sorry." Nancy shook her head.

"It's strange," Peter went on. "In my three years here I've never heard of anything like this. I mean, things occasionally get lifted in a dorm full of students, but never so many things so soon."

"Well, one thing's for sure," Nancy stated. "Whoever it is, is desperate."

"How can you tell?"

"It's just what you said: too many things too soon," she explained thoughtfully. "A good thief is patient and strikes carefully. But everyone in this dorm is on the alert. That's a desperate thief, and a desperate thief works hastily—and sloppily. Eventually, this one will make a mistake."

Fascinating and determined, Peter found himself thinking. "Well, I'm sure you'll stop it," he said.

"Me?" Nancy exclaimed, acting offended. "What makes you think I'm going to be the one to catch the thief?"

"You just strike me as the take-charge type," Peter explained. A troubled look crossed Nancy's face. "But the question is," he slipped in suggestively, holding out his cue stick, "can you play pool as well as you do everything else?"

Nancy glanced eagerly at the pool table. She said with a competitive glint in her eye, "You're on."

Peter rolled his eyes. "You sure you know what you're getting yourself into?"

For a split second Peter's eyes locked on Nancy's, and he could swear that—boyfriend or no boyfriend—she was feeling exactly the same thing he was. And whatever that thing was, it was strong, undeniable, and had nothing to do with pool. . . .

"You break," Peter dared her, snapping out of it.

As Nancy walked behind him to lean over the

table, she brushed against his back. And involuntarily Peter felt a charge all the way through to his fingertips.

Relax, he reminded himself. She's taken. And so are you, in more ways than you want to admit.

Nancy not only sank two balls on the break, but after pacing around the table, fired in two more and then a third. All the while, Peter couldn't keep his eyes off her. As much as he tried, he couldn't do it.

Finally Nancy missed.

"Not bad," Peter said. "You wouldn't be related to Minnesota Fats, the famous pool shark, would you?"

"I've never been to Minnesota," Nancy replied with a gleam in her eye.

Again an awkward silence fell between them.

Then Nancy shifted, and Peter noticed her heart-shaped gold earrings. A gift from the boyfriend, he guessed.

"I hope those beautiful earrings are real gold, or they could turn your earlobes green," he quipped.

Nancy froze, and a strange light came into her eyes, as if she'd just figured something out that had been nagging her.

She snapped her fingers. "That's it," she murmured excitedly, staring abstractly over his shoulder.

Peter looked behind him, puzzled, then turned back to Nancy. "What's it?"

Nancy's eyes came back into focus and locked

on his. "What you just said about my ears turning green."

"Earlobes," Peter said. "But that was a joke."

"But it doesn't have to be," Nancy replied, squinting, trying to remember something. "Bill . . ." she murmured. "Peter, what's that R.A.'s name on your floor?"

"Bill Graham?"

"Graham, right. And didn't he say he's a chemistry major?"

"I think so," Peter began, "but why—"

Suddenly he found Nancy's pool cue in his hands.

"I have to go," she said breathlessly.

"What is it? What did I say?" he called out as Nancy strode purposefully for the door.

"I don't have time to explain," she said. "But you gave me an idea. And if it works, maybe, just maybe, you'll get your laptop back, and your summer research won't have been wasted after all."

Staring after her as she hurried out, Peter was sorry he didn't have a chance to thank her. He felt happier than before. Confused, maybe, but happy. And he didn't think it was just the thought of getting his summer biology project back.

George's head was throbbing from her Tuesday morning lecture in her very first college class, Intro to Western Philosophy—Socrates & Associates.

She was standing in the back of the lecture hall, straining to see the blackboard and checking out the other students. A few of them were clustered at the front of the room, interrogating the professor about the first assignment. The others, like her, who either signed up for the course just to get a taste or because it was the only thing that fit in their schedule, were scattered around the room, dazed.

George glanced down at her very first college notes and sighed. They looked like a Chicago city bus map, with topics and subtopics connected by a snarl of arrows, diagrams, stars, and lines.

She moved out of the room with the others, determined to get to the bookstore so she could start on her reading. She had called her parents, who had wired her more money for her books until her money was sorted out with the state. The fact was, though the professor's lecture about truth and morality was confusing, it was also fascinating. She wanted to know more.

As she moved outside with the swarm of students, she thought she heard someone call her name. Shielding her eyes, she squinted into the sharp late-morning sunshine and saw an unmistakable silhouette: tall and lean, with beautiful, silky black hair. "Will," she whispered, and fought her way toward him.

"How'd it go?" he asked.

"It's hard," George replied. "But it's interesting."

"The only things worth doing in life are hard," Will said.

Something about his tone of voice convinced George that he knew this from experience.

"How about a cup of coffee?" he asked hopefully. "I talked so much about me yesterday that I woke up this morning realizing I didn't learn much about you."

George glanced at her watch and frowned. "I have to get to the bookstore—and then I have to do battle with the U.S. government. I'm going to be an official draft dodger in about forty-eight hours, and then the only coffee I'll be drinking will be a special blend of prison brew. Also I need to battle the state to get my money for books and supplies."

An admiring glint came to Will's eye. "I like your spirit," he said. "But I don't mind waiting. How long will it take?"

"Our private phone isn't hooked up yet," George explained, "so I have to wait in line at the pay phones. And who knows how long that will take—not to mention all my quarters."

Will smiled broadly. He leaned down and lifted George's book bag off her shoulder. Laughing, she tried to yank it back, but she was no match for him—not that she tried very hard. "What're you doing?" she asked.

"Habit," Will said. "My father taught me well." And he began to walk away.

"But where are we going?" George asked, falling in beside him.

"Waterman Street."

"What's that?"

"There's an intimate little place there called Café Blackfeather."

George stopped in her tracks. "Will, I really have to get these things done."

"Don't worry." Will laughed. "I have an espresso machine in my apartment. And I have this cool new invention called the telephone. It doesn't take quarters, but it does take invitations to dinner. What do you say?"

George's heart was pounding. He's too good to be true, she told herself. Am I really interesting to him?

This was the very last thing she expected to happen to her—and so soon. But she'd be lying if she said she hadn't hoped.

"But I don't want to bother you with this, Will," she protested. "You've got better things to do."

Will's smiling eyes sobered. "My family is well-practiced at dealing with the government," he said pensively. "You don't get what you want from them unless you fight for it."

"But it might take all afternoon."

"An afternoon with you?" Will said, his mood lightening again. "I'll take it. And we'll get your problems solved—I promise."

"Okay," George agreed, "but after the bookstore?"

Will nodded. "After the bookstore."

"Then let's go," she said excitedly, leading him on. "To battle!"

Will punched the air in anticipation. "To battle!"

Across the quad, Nancy was flying down the steps of Smith Hall. Her first journalism class had just ended, and her blood was pumping so hard she thought her veins would burst. The professor was a retired war correspondent who'd defied everyone from presidents to generals to get the "untold story."

Journalism was about prying apart the obvious and the known, he told the class: the truth of anything lies below the surface. After his short lecture, he showed the class a documentary about journalists during the Vietnam War. In a democracy, he said, journalists are more than just reporters, they are America's conscience.

Thinking about the notice she'd seen about Wednesday night's meeting for new staff for the *Wilder Times,* Nancy peered up into the endless sky. Excitedly, she saw her years at Wilder stretch out before her: they were full of hope and potential, filled with all the things she hadn't done yet and all the stories she had yet to write. She knew in her heart that journalism was for her.

"What a perfect beginning to college life," she said out loud.

As she crossed the quad, Nancy glanced at the clock tower. It was eleven o'clock. In two hours she was supposed to meet with Bill at the chemistry building to discuss her plan for catching the thief.

Nancy laughed at herself. A stolen locket may not be a war, she mused, but after all, I'm only a freshman.

She thought of the next two hours she had to kill: Let's see—I have most of my books, and I don't really have enough time to start on my reading. . . . Then it came to her—Bess.

Wow, she thought. It feels like weeks since I've seen her. This would be a great time to talk to her about her roommate troubles.

While she headed for Jamison Hall, she thought that once she stopped the thief, she might begin plotting out an exposé about unpublicized crime at Wilder University. That would really impress the editors.

"It's me, Bess," Nancy called as she knocked on the door to Bess's room. But as soon as her knuckle hit wood, the door swung open. Nancy poked her head in, surprised.

"I'm glad you're in, Bess—" Nancy began, but what she saw made the words catch in her throat.

Stepping into the room, Nancy walked over to Bess's bed. She sat down and placed a hand gently on Bess's back. It wasn't much of a surprise that Bess hardly noticed. She was lying facedown, sobbing uncontrollably.

This can't just be roommate trouble, Nancy finally realized. This is something much worse, and I haven't been here for her.

CHAPTER 12

"You want to tell me about it?" Nancy asked softly as she propped her friend up on her bed. Bess raised her tear-streaked face.

"I've been trying to tell you and George since Sunday morning," she cried, "but I can never find you. You're either on the phone or you're off at some party without me. It's like I'm not important anymore."

"Bess," Nancy said, horrified. "You know that's not true." Nancy couldn't believe what she was hearing. It was true that she'd been busy, and she guessed that George was, too. But why wasn't Bess? In fact, if she and George had one worry about Bess, it was that she would be so busy socializing and partying that she would never have time to study. Never in a million years had Nancy thought that Bess would wind up sobbing in her arms on the first day of classes. Never.

"Bess," Nancy said evenly. She lifted her old

friend's chin in her hand and peered into her eyes. "You and George are the best friends I have in the world. There's something going on that's been taking up a lot of my time. But I don't care about that now. *You're* what's important. I want you to talk to me."

"Do you remember that guy Dave?" Bess said, wiping her face with the back of her hands. "The one who asked me to the Zeta party?"

"I saw you dancing," Nancy said. "Before I left the party, I couldn't find you. I figured you'd tell me about it later."

"I tried," Bess whispered. "Sunday morning—"

"In my room," Nancy said. "I know. But Ned called—I'm really sorry. Things aren't going great with us right now. But never mind about that. So"—she sat back, expecting to hear another tale of unrequited love—"this is about Dave?"

Bess didn't move. Something about the faraway expression in her eyes worried Nancy. No, this wasn't about a crush. This was something worse.

"Bess, what aren't you telling me?" Nancy asked.

The floodgates opened again, and Bess leaned against Nancy, sobbing onto her shoulder. "I don't know," she said over and over again. "I think it was my fault."

Nancy grabbed Bess by the shoulders and held her at arm's length, searching her face for answers. "Did that creep do something to you?"

"Almost," Bess whimpered. "But I got away."

For the next fifteen minutes Nancy listened quietly as Bess told her about following Dave up to his room, his trying to kiss her, about her running away just in time, and how it had affected everything she'd done since then. Then she talked about Brian, who was the first guy she'd met who treated her like a friend and not a sex object.

When Bess fell silent, Nancy took her friend's hands in her own and held them. "Bess, look at me," she insisted. "Whatever happened with Dave, it wasn't your fault. Do you understand?"

"It isn't? Right?" Bess whispered.

"Absolutely not," Nancy stated resolutely. "Maybe you shouldn't have gone upstairs with him, but just because you did doesn't mean he could do whatever he wanted to you."

For the first time Nancy saw a flicker of a smile come to Bess's face.

"I guess I'm lucky nothing really bad happened, huh?" Bess said.

Nancy nodded. "You are."

"So what do I do?" Bess asked.

Nancy thought a minute. "This guy definitely sounds like a real creep," she finally said. "But the fact is, you got away before he did anything, so it's probably not worth going to the police. So maybe you should just tell your R.A. about it," Nancy suggested. "She'll know what to do. But keep your eyes and ears open. The second you hear that he did this to anyone else, we'll go to the police."

Bess nodded.

"And promise me one more thing," Nancy said.

Bess looked at her expectantly.

"Tell George about what happened. The three of us have always been friends, and we always will be. No secrets."

"No secrets," Bess echoed, smiling. "And we'll go to a party together soon?"

"Count on it," Nancy said firmly.

As Nancy left Jamison Hall and headed toward the chemistry building, she knew something had been changed forever. What had happened to Bess, and what was happening between her and Ned, were the signs of their growing up. Growing up and growing apart. They were starting a new phase of their lives, and who could say how they'd end up? But we'll always be close, she reflected.

Nancy headed down to the basement, as Bill had directed, and walked the length of the dim hallway lined with narrow, windowless doors. She stopped at the end of the hall and turned to the unmarked door on the right.

Nancy knocked twice. The door opened a crack, and Bill stood in the doorway—totally transformed from the Bill she had met at the party the other night. He was wearing a long white lab coat, his expression deadly serious.

"Do you have it?" Nancy asked.

Bill looked over Nancy's shoulder checking to

see if the coast was clear. Then he produced a small package wrapped in plain brown paper.

"Don't touch this stuff with your bare hands," he cautioned. "And no matter what happens, don't tell anyone where you got it. I'd be risking my research grant if this got out."

"I understand," Nancy assured him.

"Good luck," Bill said, then shut the door.

"Thanks," Nancy murmured. "I'll need it."

How exciting—a suite meeting just about me. What's Dawn saying now? To always lock our doors, to keep an eye out for strangers in the hall. Brilliant plan. What an original thinker.

What's that? You want us to start an around-the-clock watch, everybody gets a two-hour shift? Give me a break.

That's right, everyone go ahead and groan. Can't you guys see that I don't like doing this? None of you in this room knows what I'm going through. It's too late to stop, though. Besides, I'm not taking anything any of you can't live without. You have money. I have needs.

Hey! What's that new necklace Nancy's wearing? Family heirloom, huh?

Wow! It's really nice. Funny, I missed it the first time. That looks like a tiny diamond hanging off the gold chain. Must be worth a lot. If I could get my hands on that . . .

Nancy just told Ginny she'd hide it in her room. Perfect, huh? Yeah. Perfect for me!

* * *

Nancy sat hunched over in a study carrel in the library. Her eyes strayed from the textbook in front of her to the wall clock for perhaps the twentieth time in the last fifteen minutes. She sighed heavily, nerves and anticipation making her jumpy. She could almost swear the clock wasn't moving.

After the meeting in the lounge had broken up, she'd made a point of loudly mentioning that she was off to the library for her first bout with college-level homework.

What luck that Ginny had asked if she meant to wear her heirloom necklace with all the stealing going on. Nancy had been able to announce to everyone that she'd leave it behind in her room, in a wonderful hiding place.

Nancy remembered that Stephanie kept staring at her necklace. She seemed very interested. And she'd rushed off as soon as the meeting ended. Well, if it is Stephanie, Nancy thought, we'll know soon enough.

Her trap was set, thanks to Bill, and even more, thanks to Dawn's surprise suite meeting. It was the perfect opportunity for her to plant the bait. She'd drawn as much attention to herself as she'd thought safe. Now all she could do was sit and wait—and hope.

How much longer should I give it? Nancy wondered impatiently, loudly drumming her fingers on her book.

Someone down the aisle cleared his throat.

"Sorry," Nancy murmured, and forced her eyes

back down to the words. Surely the Civil War was much more important than a petty thief. But she couldn't keep her mind focused.

Suddenly she remembered her pool match with Peter. "I'm sure you'll catch him," he'd said confidently. Nancy hoped Peter was right. Only she was pretty positive that it wasn't a *him* at all.

After impatiently waiting another fifteen minutes, Nancy closed her books and stuffed them into her backpack. As she left the study carrel, she noticed that all around her students were sitting down to begin their studies, starting their careers as college students. All Nancy could hope as she pushed her way out the library doors was that someone else's career was about to end.

The steaming hot water spilled from the tap as she furiously scrubbed at her hands.

Off, off, off, her mind screamed. *Get it off before everyone comes back!*

She'd lathered half a bar of soap, but the purple stains on her fingers weren't disappearing.

She was sweating. All she could think about was getting herself clean. Then she heard someone at the door behind her. And suddenly the noise of the faucet became a roar in her ears.

She couldn't take her hands out from the hot water. They hung limply in front of her, the purple stains showing like a bruise, or blood. In the mirror she watched the knob turn and wondered fleetingly why she hadn't locked it. It wouldn't have mattered this time, she realized.

The door swung in behind her, and her gaze rose, up past the slim jeans and the black T-shirt. She found herself staring into Nancy's eyes. Bright blue eyes that expressed her surprise, and then her sadness.

She watched Nancy's lips move and heard the soft voice that seemed to bounce off the mirror. "So, are you going to tell me about it?"

CHAPTER 13

Julie, maybe we should sit in my room and talk this over," Nancy said firmly.

Nancy left the door to her room partially open behind them. Julie was leaning against the darkened window, her fingers pressed against the glass.

Nancy could see her shoulders shaking and could hear her crying softly. She looks so helpless, Nancy thought. But she knew she had to keep her feelings in check. Julie didn't mind stealing from her friends, she reminded herself.

Finally Julie turned around, her eyes red, her lips trembling. "You're not going to call the police, are you?" she whimpered.

"Why don't you sit down," Nancy said.

Julie almost collapsed onto Nancy's bed.

"Okay, I'm listening," Nancy said, folding her arms across her chest.

Julie looked up, her face tear streaked, like a

window in the rain. "Why should I say anything?"

"Because I'm the most sympathetic person you're going to find right now," Nancy replied.

"But you won't believe me."

"Try me," Nancy said.

"I didn't keep the money," Julie said.

"You're right. I don't believe you."

"Well, I didn't keep *all* of it. I used it."

"For?" Nancy prodded.

"Sometimes I need a little help, you know?"

Nancy shook her head. "No, I don't know."

Julie was jittery, wringing her hands and tapping her feet. "Well, I need—" she began. "A little energy when I'm down, and a little something to relax when I'm too hyped up."

"Like right now," Nancy said.

"Yeah," Julie admitted. "A little pill, a downer, or something to even me out, get me through."

Julie began to shiver with fear. She looked up at Nancy with pleading eyes. "I know I need help, Nancy. But I don't have anywhere to go!"

"You've never talked to your parents?" Nancy asked.

"My parents!" Julie almost laughed. "They wouldn't understand. It would kill them."

Nancy sat on the bed next to Julie. "But don't you see you're killing yourself," she said.

"I promised myself I'd get help after the semester was over. You know, go home and dry out and start over next term." Julie lowered her face to her hands and began to sob. "It doesn't matter now," she wept. "I'm a goner."

Nancy heard footsteps outside the door and raised her head.

"Knock, knock," called a voice from the hall.

Nancy stood up quickly to intercept the visitor, but then Dawn's smiling face appeared in the crack of the door. "Nancy? I thought I heard someone crying in here. Are you all right?"

"You'd better come in," Nancy said, letting Dawn in and locking the door behind her.

"Julie!" Dawn exclaimed. "What happened? Was something of yours stolen?"

Julie, her face twisted with confusion and pain, glanced up at Nancy.

"Do you want to tell her or should I?" Nancy asked.

"Tell me what?" Dawn asked worriedly, turning from one to the other.

"You'd better sit down," Nancy said, sitting again on the bed. Dawn lowered herself into Nancy's desk chair. "It seems that Julie has been working overtime," Nancy said. A puzzled look swept across Dawn's eyes. "Julie's the one we've been looking for," Nancy explained sorrowfully.

Dawn's jaw dropped. *"You're* the thief?" she whispered. "But I don't understand. How? Why?" She was too stunned to talk.

"I'll explain later how she was caught," Nancy began. "But right now we need to get Julie to talk about it."

Julie took her hands away from her face. Her

teeth were chattering, her nose was running. She looked ready to come apart at the seams.

"I'm not a drug addict, like the ones you see in the street," she cried indignantly. "And I'm not a hardened criminal, either."

"We never said you were," Nancy said, trying to soothe her.

Julie softened. "You have to understand," she whispered. "It's the only way I can get through the day."

"Wait," Dawn interrupted. "You stole to get money for drugs?"

Julie's head bobbed with quick little nods.

"But why? Since when?" Dawn asked.

Julie shrugged. "High school, I guess. Things were cool, but they were too easy. I don't know. I guess I was bored. I started drinking at parties, and pretty soon I drank my way through classes. Then people started giving me other stuff— grass, pills.

"High school's when I found out I was talented," Julie continued.

Nancy raised an eyebrow. "Talented?"

"My allowance wasn't enough to buy me enough of the drugs I needed, so I found out I could steal and sell the stuff for cash. I could steal really well. Lift things out of stores, friends' closets—"

"Peter's laptop," Dawn gasped. She stood and began to pace back and forth in front of the window. "You ruined all of Peter's research." She turned and glared at Julie. "And you sold everything for drug money?"

"Yes, except ..." Julie hesitated, then gave Nancy a guilty look. "Except Nancy's locket. I lost it before I could sell it. I'm so sorry, Nancy."

Nancy just stared at Julie, keeping quiet for the moment about finding her locket.

"What about the computer?" Nancy asked. "Did you sell that?"

For the first time a glimmer of a smile played across Julie's lips. "I still have it."

"Well, he'll be glad to hear that," Dawn said. "That was three months of work you almost destroyed. So, everything else is gone?"

Julie nodded. "I owe a lot of money to people," she said. "The kind of people who would have hurt me."

"Julie, I can't believe this," Nancy said.

"You wouldn't understand." Julie seemed to sink back into her shell.

"I understand plenty," Dawn said authoritatively. "I understand that you belong in the hands of the police—"

Julie's eyes lit up with fear. "The police!"

"You're a criminal, Julie," Dawn stated matter-of-factly. "If you're not that, then what are you?"

Julie whimpered, "I'm a drug addict." She turned to Nancy. "Oh, Nancy!" she cried. "Do you know what would happen to me if I had to go to jail?"

Nancy had to push down her own rising anger about Julie's stealing Ned's locket.

This is about more than a piece of metal, she thought to herself. Julie's entire life is at stake. Maybe it's not too late to help.

Nancy turned to Dawn. "Do you have to turn her in?" she asked. "If Julie agrees to pay everyone back and check into a rehabilitation program, maybe we can give her a break."

"I'll do anything not to go," Julie cried.

Dawn paced the room, squinting into space in deep thought. "It's true. You need help, not just punishment," she thought aloud, waving a hand.

Finally Dawn stopped and turned to Julie. "You'll do anything?" she asked.

Julie nodded eagerly.

Nancy grabbed Julie's hand. Here was her opening. "Would you go for treatment?"

"Yes," Julie whispered, defeated.

"We're not talking about seeing a social worker once a week, Julie," Dawn declared earnestly. "We're talking about checking yourself into a hospital, for professional treatment for your addiction, and whatever else—"

Julie sighed. "I understand."

"Tomorrow," Dawn insisted.

Julie began to pout. "Tomorrow? What about school?"

"Tomorrow," Dawn commanded her. "That's the deal. Tomorrow—or I call the police. Take it or leave it."

Julie looked to Nancy.

"Take it," Nancy said to her.

"Okay," Julie sobbed, tears rolling off her cheeks and into her hands. "I'll go."

"Okay," Dawn said, heading for the door. "Let's go to my room. My phone got turned on yesterday. We can call your parents from there."

Julie swallowed hard. Her eyes widened with a panicked look. "My parents?"

"You need them now," Nancy said soothingly.

Julie shook her head. "But they won't understand."

"They'll understand," Nancy assured her, giving Julie a nod. "Trust me."

Dawn cleared her throat. "Julie, listen to me. Before I agree not to go to the police, I need to hear assurance from your parents that they'll send you to a rehab program and that everyone you stole from will be reimbursed. Ginny, for one, needs her money back quickly. And Reva's great-grandfather's watch. Can you get that back?"

"Probably," Julie said with a reluctant nod. "I know who has it." She stood up and seemed to waver on her feet. Nancy rushed forward to prop her up, but Julie held up her hand. She looked at Nancy with tortured, reddened eyes. "I'm okay," she said quietly. "I've got to start standing up on my own sometime."

"I'm glad to hear it," Nancy said.

"And, Nancy?" Julie said weakly. "I'm really sorry about the locket. I'm sorry—"

Nancy interrupted her. "Actually, Julie, someone found my locket and returned it to me."

Julie looked relieved, then a new batch of tears began spilling out of her eyes. "I'm so sorry about everything. I really liked you. I really liked all of you. It wasn't anything personal."

Nancy sympathetically rested a hand on Julie's shoulder and smiled, trying to be cheerful. "What'll make it up to us is to see you get better, Julie. Just work hard and get yourself well. Who knows, maybe we'll see you back at Wilder very soon."

For a second Julie seemed to brighten. "Yeah, maybe," she said. Then her face darkened again, and her lips began to tremble. "You'll tell the others I'm really sorry?"

"Of course," Nancy said with a nod.

"Ready to make that call?" Dawn stepped in.

"Ready as I'll ever be," Julie sniffed.

"It's hard to imagine what it must have been like for her," Dawn said later as she and Nancy sat in the deserted cafeteria, talking over Julie's story.

"Yeah," Nancy agreed. "It's hard to think about turning someone in to the authorities when she has a problem like that. And I think the choice you gave her was really fair."

"I think it was best for her, anyway," Dawn said. "It's a good thing all the girls in the suite agreed not to press charges as long as they got their things back."

"Her parents were cool about everything?" Nancy asked.

Dawn shook her head. "They were really amazing. They took the news really well. Mr. Hammerman said he suspected Julie had a problem but was waiting for her to come to him. And Mrs. Hammerman talked to Julie for a whole hour, and then got on the phone with me and said she was coming right away to get her. Right now," Dawn said, holding up her watch, "Julie should be checking into a clinic near their home."

"I wonder who her supplier is," Nancy mused aloud.

"That was one piece of information she just refused to give. She said he was dangerous and would find a way to get back at her."

"But if he's not found, sooner or later someone's going to get hurt. That girl who OD'd Saturday night is lucky to be alive."

"I heard some talk that there's a guy in the Zeta frat who has a reputation for getting people drugs," Dawn said. "Maybe Julie's supplier was his contact, or maybe the guy in Zeta is Julie's supplier."

Dawn sighed, exhausted. "I still can't believe I missed the warning signs Julie was giving. From what you've said, her mood swings were enormous. I should have seen it sooner."

"You can't blame yourself," Nancy argued. "Your job doesn't include following us around all day."

"Maybe not," Dawn agreed, "but I've also had other things on my mind—things that should have taken second place to my responsibilities as an R.A."

Nancy knew that Dawn was talking about Peter, and she didn't know quite what to say.

"So how exactly did you figure it out?" Dawn asked quickly, turning the conversation away from herself. "Did you suspect Julie all this time? I never would have guessed."

"Actually," Nancy said, "I thought it was Stephanie."

Dawn looked up, surprised.

"It's probably because I don't like her very much," Nancy admitted with an embarrassed smile. "Also, Julie kept dropping hints about Stephanie's being the thief. Now, of course, it makes sense that Julie was trying to throw suspicion onto someone else. But at our suite meeting, Stephanie seemed very interested in my new necklace when I was talking about it with Ginny and Reva. Oh, and there's that strange, high-security padlock Stephanie has on her dresser drawer."

"Lock?" Dawn raised an eyebrow. "Why would she need a lock? Should I be concerned?"

Nancy laughed. "Not about the lock, anyway. While you and Julie were on the phone with the Hammermans, Stephanie came back and I asked her about it."

"What did she say?" Dawn asked anxiously.

" 'None of your business,' " Nancy said, imitating Stephanie's cool, dismissive tone. " 'Can't someone get some privacy around here?' "

Nancy waved her hand. "Stephanie's Stephanie. Who knows what she has in there? Whatever it is, I'm sure it's pretty harmless, just like her."

Dawn laughed. "I have to hand it to you, Drew. You're pretty perceptive. But how *did* you figure out that it was Julie?"

"I didn't really, until I saw her in the bathroom. That necklace I had on wasn't real," Nancy explained. "It was also coated in a chemical solution that reacts with the natural acids in human skin." Nancy winked. "Basically, it stains worse than tomato sauce."

Dawn nodded. "So that's what that purple stuff was all over her hands. Where did you get something like that? I didn't think you were a chem major."

"I'm not, actually," Nancy said. "A friend helped me."

Dawn nodded. Then her eyes lit up. "A friend with a research grant, I'll bet." She smiled knowingly.

Nancy grinned. Dawn was smart. Obviously not very much could get past her. The more time they spent together, Nancy realized, the more she liked her.

If only that wasn't such a problem, Nancy sighed, sipping her coffee. If only I didn't find Dawn's boyfriend so attractive.

CHAPTER 14

"It's really nice to be hanging out with you two on campus," Bess said happily, sitting between Nancy and George on the steps of Smith Hall after Wednesday morning classes.

The quad was full of students walking the paths between buildings and streaming in and out of the doors.

"You seem happy," George said. "Did you have Leslie kidnapped or something?"

"You mean the human ice cube?" Bess replied. "I wish. I still can't believe she told me you brought over that invitation after I'd already left for that party, Nancy. Why would she make that up?"

Nancy and George locked eyes and said, in unison, "Jealousy!"

Bess shook her head. "Well, I'm glad you two understand her."

"Maybe you should get her out into the sun and warm her up," Nancy suggested.

"Yeah, and then it'll start snowing." Bess snickered.

She tilted her face toward the sun, feeling better than she had in days and days. "How much time do we have before the next class?"

"Exactly seven minutes," George said, checking her watch. "Seven minutes until Calculus 112, the notoriously difficult freshman prereq. At least, I have a book for it. I'm so glad my parents sent me more money in time. I still have a little problem of draft dodging to overcome, but I know it'll be solved soon."

"I'm glad you're taking calculus this semester and getting it over with," Nancy teased, catching Bess's eye. "That way you'll be able to help us in the spring."

"Oh, sure," George replied. "But unfortunately, I hope to be part of the track and field team in the spring, and I just may not have the time."

Bess turned to her wide-eyed.

"Hey," George said, "you can have my notes."

"You'll be giving me more than just notes, cousin," Bess threatened good-naturedly. "I'd like your undivided attention as my personal tutor, pal, and best cousin on the planet."

"Nice try"—George shook her head—"but compliments will get you nowhere."

"Well, I can get you to your next class if you're ready, Bess," a voice quipped.

Bess smiled when she saw Brian standing before them. She could sense both George and

Nancy eyeing him, and she almost laughed. They were just like her parents or something—thank heaven.

"Brian, this is my cousin George and my friend Nancy," she said.

"Nice to meet you both." He bowed low. "I hope I'll get a chance to spend more time with you, but right now we'd better get moving. We don't want to be late for Psych 120, right, Bess? Aren't we just dying to find out what makes us chronically confused, late, and averse to higher technology?"

Nancy and George burst out laughing, and Bess grinned.

"But you have to promise me one thing," Brian continued.

"Anything," Bess said boldly, knowing that Nancy and George were throwing each other meaningful glances.

"There's an audition for the Drama Department's first production of the year," Brian said, a challenging glint in his eye. "And since I know how disappointed you were to be shut out of Intro to Drama"—he paused—"I went ahead and signed us both up."

"Great," Nancy cried.

"You sure you can memorize the lines?" George teased.

"Of course she can," Brian said enthusiastically. "I've already seen her do a very moving portrayal of a suffering heroine. Now I think she should try her hand as a comic actress."

Even though she'd auditioned in front of a roomful of people numerous times in the past, for some reason the thought of doing it here, in college, instantly made Bess's stomach clench. But when she looked into Brian's supportive eyes, she felt calmed.

"Don't you laugh, George Fayne and Nancy Drew," she said, picking up her backpack and linking her arm with Brian's. "This girl is going to survive freshman year after all, and why shouldn't I get a standing ovation or two on the way?"

After the day's classes were over, Nancy stepped through the suite door and collapsed onto the couch in the lounge with her book bag, realizing too late that she was so exhausted she might never lift herself out.

Everything had started to take its toll. Now that the thief was caught and she understood what had upset Bess so much, her defenses were down: she could feel again. And what she felt was absolutely drained.

She closed her eyes and fell into a half sleep. She thought she heard someone sobbing, then decided she must be dreaming. *It's just Julie. I'm feeling guilty about sending her away. It was her problem, not yours. If anything, you may have saved her life.*

Nancy woke up. But the sobs weren't fading. Her eyes followed the sound and she found herself staring at Dawn's door.

By some miracle, Nancy got off the couch and knocked.

The door was thrown open and Dawn filled the doorway, her makeup blotchy and streaked with tears, her nose red, her eyes puffy.

"Oh, Nancy, it's you," Dawn said unenthusiastically. "I thought it might be Peter."

Then she stepped back and sank down onto her bed.

"May I come in?" Nancy asked.

Dawn gestured to her chair and tried to pull herself together. She held her breath to stop herself from crying. But all she did was make herself hiccup, which at least made her laugh.

Nancy smiled with relief. "Do you want to talk about it?"

"Why not?" Dawn shrugged. "You'll find out sooner or later. It's about Peter. He broke up with me last night."

"Oh, Dawn, I'm sorry," Nancy said.

"Not as sorry as I am," Dawn replied, and quickly reached for a tissue. "I'm sorry I'm so pathetically weepy," she continued, "but you know how people have the love of their life, the one person in the world who will make them happy, their soul mate?"

I thought I did, Nancy answered to herself. To Dawn, she nodded, encouraging her to get it all off her chest.

"Well, I thought Peter was mine. We've been together since last spring. But the closer we got, the more he seemed to push me away. Then, these last couple of days, I don't know what happened. He said the relationship was getting too serious for him. He couldn't handle it, because he didn't think he could love me the way I love him, and that we should stop seeing each other."

Dawn gazed deeply into Nancy's eyes as if the answer she was looking for was written there. "He was my one chance for being with the perfect man. And now he's gone . . ."

Nancy let Dawn take her hand and squeeze it. But she herself was far away. As if by itself, as if her heart separated from her mind, some piece of her began to think about Ned. Where was he? Was he in the library studying? Was he playing pool with his friends? She couldn't see him.

Who *is* Ned in my life? she wondered. I can't picture him. Is this what happens—the clearer things should be getting, the more complicated they are?

Dawn was talking to her, and Nancy hadn't heard a thing.

"Well?" Dawn asked, waiting. "Do you know, Nancy?"

"No," Nancy said—it seemed the safest answer.

Dawn nodded knowingly. "You're right. I don't know what love means, either. One minute you're laughing together, you're best friends. He tells you he loves you. And then"—she snapped her fingers—"he's gone. And he just doesn't love you anymore. If you figure it out, let me know."

Half an hour later Nancy left Dawn sleeping

and went to her own room. She had a few minutes before she had to leave for the first staff meeting of the *Wilder Times*. A nap, even a short one, sounded great.

As she opened the door, she saw a small square of paper lying on her pillow. For some reason, she wasn't surprised when she picked it up and saw that it was a message from Ned. He'd called around noon and wanted her to call him back—it was important.

Nancy looked at the message for a solid minute, then sat at her desk and scanned the contents. Her eyes snagged on Ned's photo. She picked it up and held it in the palm of her hand, as if weighing it—as if weighing *him*, weighing the past.

Nancy blinked, and in that millisecond her entire relationship with Ned Nickerson passed before her eyes: high school, the feel of his sweaty palm when they first held hands, their first kiss, their endless talks, the endless laughter.

Endless? Nancy wondered, close to tears. Maybe it's not endless. Maybe there's an end to everything.

Nancy glanced at her watch and stood. I can't think about this right now, she decided. She was exhausted, but the idea of working for the campus newspaper excited her so much. After all, it was her future. She had enough energy for this one last thing, this meeting.

Turning to leave, she dropped the square of paper with Ned's message, and it floated and rocked, like a falling leaf, onto her desk. Ned would have to wait. The tug-of-war of competing emotions was pulling her heart every which way.

Downstairs, Nancy strode across the lobby. She didn't fail to say hello to the new acquaintances she passed.

And she didn't fail to smile as she stepped through the door into the orange, late afternoon sunshine.

NEXT IN NANCY DREW ON CAMPUS™:

Life at Wilder University is proving to be full of surprises and scandal. Bess is beginning to think that Brian Daglian is different from all the guys she's gone out with before... and she's about to find out why. And George has been asked out by the most popular guy around—quarterback Scooter Berenson—only to end up the most hated person on campus! Nancy, meanwhile, has signed on with *Wilder Times*, the university paper, and she may soon break a story about Scooter that could leave him in disgrace... or even in danger. But first she must deal with Ned, who's coming up for the weekend. And the way she's feeling about her new life, his visit could mark the biggest break of all... in *On Her Own*, Nancy Drew on Campus #2.

For everyone who believes— a romantic and suspenseful new trilogy

KISSED BY AN ANGEL

by Elizabeth Chandler

When Ivy loses her boyfriend, Tristan, in a car accident, she also loses her faith in angels. But Tristan is now an angel himself, desperately trying to protect Ivy. Only the power of love can save her...and set her free to love again.

Volume I

Kissed by an Angel

Volume II

The Power of Love

Volume III

Soulmates

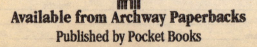

Available from Archway Paperbacks
Published by Pocket Books

1110